MORE DOGS

AND THEIR TWISTED TALES—
AND ONE CAT STORY

AMY KRISTOFF

Deer Run Press
Cushing, Maine

Library of Congress Card Number: 2017963725

ISBN: 978-1-937869-07-6

First Printing, 2018, USA

Published by
Deer Run Press
8 Cushing Road
Cushing, ME 04563

Contents

Getting What He Deserves

You'd think picking up your dog from the groomer's would be totally uneventful—but for Mira, she met her future husband that way. His undoing was failing to like dogs as much as she did. He could have "learned to like" her Sheltie, Ollie, whom she'd rescued from a pet shop. Before it was over, Eric made no secret of detesting her dog (and dogs in general). That hurt worse than him wanting a divorce. (But she didn't mind being the one to initiate the proceedings.)

Mira had dropped off Ollie at eight in the morning at "Doggie Suds," located in "Goldust Crossing" strip mall in Scottsdale, Arizona. He was never ready before two and she got off work at three, so she didn't have to wait around. She would go in the grooming salon "dressed up" because of her job, so perhaps she'd unwittingly been attracting attention. She didn't even look like the same person without doing her hair and make-up.

As far as Ollie, Mira had him groomed every three weeks, and she had him shaved when the weather started to get warm. She was very particular about keeping her two-bedroom condo clean, and she'd never owned a dog before acquiring Ollie. It was sheer luck the homeowner's association allowed dogs. The last thing she would have wanted to do was move. The location of the condominium development was quite unique, located a quarter mile from a scenic wayside with an impressive drop-off and a view of downtown Phoenix in the distance.

"Loneliness and boredom" were what had compelled Mira to acquire a canine companion. It was lame of her to go to a pet shop in a Mesa mega-mall to appease her desire, but that was the case. It had been effortless to take pity on the five-month-old Sheltie whose price was reduced. Mira was reduced to tears and had to have him, even though she hardly had an ideal living arrangement for such a hyperactive dog. As an administrator for the private Coachella Valley Day School, she had a five-day work week, plenty of vacation time and summers off. She walked Ollie twice a day during the week and up to four times a day over the weekend. Some of those walks included going to the scenic overlook and back. Unfailingly Mira had to pull Ollie back from the precipice. There was a heavy wire barrier, but he still could have slipped through and acted hell-bent on doing so.

Just as Mira was about to open the passenger door of her white Jeep Patriot for Ollie to hop in, a man asked from behind her, "Miss, may I pet your beautiful dog for a minute?"

"O.K.," she replied before even having the opportunity to see who asked the question. Then she turned around and was wowed. He was tall, dark-haired, mid-thirties like herself. Mira had quit men dose to six years ago, thanks to a horrendous relationship that went on too long. She decided if she couldn't pick the right kind of guy she wouldn't date at all. Ollie had become such an integral part of her life, it was impossible to say she was lonely.

Before she knew it, Mira was shifting Ollie's leash to her other hand and shaking hands with "Eric Gerber." He was honored to meet her and without hesitation invited her to join him for coffee at "Coffee Haus," which was two doors down from Doggie Suds.

At the coffee shop there was seating "en plein air," in comfortable, round-backed, green metal chairs. Mira was glad Ollie could accompany them, not only because she didn't want to leave him in her Patriot (even though it wasn't hot out), but he needed more socialization. Besides, if Ollie didn't like Eric, this might be an opportunity to find out as much.

Mira ordered an espresso and Eric ordered black coffee. Ollie sat to her right, not avoiding Eric but definitely not interested in sitting between them. Did that mean Ollie was "neutral" about him?

The first question Mira asked Eric was, "Do you have a dog?"

"No, I don't," he replied. "With all the hours I work, I honestly don't have time for one. My mom has a dog I take care of when she goes away, which is quite often these days. She's gotten into doing some traveling after my dad passed away a couple years ago."

"I'm sorry to hear that."

"Thank you. He was ill for quite a long time, which was hard on my mom because she took care of him until everything became too much and she had to hire some in-home nurse's help."

Of course Mira's sympathies were already in overdrive for Eric, a man she didn't even know but couldn't get enough of his gentlemanliness and good looks and apparent interest in her and her dog. What was there not to like about him? Maybe her elation was due to the fact it had been a long time since she'd been on a date, not that this even was one.

Mira gave Eric her phone number and agreed to see him again. She left things at that and pretended to be coy by not asking for his number. She'd been burned too many times to get overly excited about a guy right away. As it was, she barely knew anything about him, although they did chat for about forty-five minutes. He ended things by abruptly standing and declaring, "I won't take up any more of your time." Everything he did made an impression on her, despite her not wanting to let it do so. She couldn't help herself!

As Mira was driving home with Ollie, she went over the

meeting with Eric. A troubling thing he'd said was in response to a question she'd asked whether he'd had a dog, growing up. His response was: "My family did when I was really young, but it had some health problems, so it was put to sleep. My parents acted like they made it disappear, as if that would spare me from any grief. Doing that messed with my head."

Another disquieting factor about "the date" was Eric virtually disappeared upon leaving Coffee Haus and didn't even bother walking Mira and Ollie to her vehicle. Maybe she was being needlessly picky. Or maybe he seemed to be too good to be true, so she was looking for an excuse to criticize him. It was definitely troubling he appeared to think nothing of referring to a dog he was familiar with as "it."

As excited as Mira was to have met Eric, she wasn't about to start taking Ollie's presence for granted. Having him in her life was everything, despite their rocky start together. Fortunately in the past year he'd mellowed out a lot, and she was proud of herself for persevering. Meanwhile, more than one dumped ex-boyfriend had the nerve to accuse her of not trying hard enough to make their relationship work.

Mira got home with Ollie and let him out in the small backyard. Then she put away the bag of groceries she'd purchased at a gourmet shop. Barely did she finish the task and her mobile phone rang. The number read as "unknown," but she answered it anyway. It was Eric! She was shamelessly thrilled, relieved, etc. After greetings were quickly exchanged, he said, "I know you probably just got home, but I couldn't wait. I'd like to have you over to my place for dinner. I'm not like a super-great cook, but I pride myself on making 'the effort.' Please don't take this the wrong way and think I'm being pushy."

"No, I don't," Mira told him, although she wasn't being entirely truthful. Since she didn't know him, what was wrong with not being comfortable going to his place for dinner? She wasn't in as much of a hurry to date again as she originally thought. The reasonable thing to do next was go online and see if she could dig up any information on him. Or maybe she was better off not knowing.

Somehow Mira got to the next afternoon at work before it occurred to her she was "going to a stranger's for dinner tonight." She hadn't dared tell a soul (not even—or especially?) her mother. Possibly she liked to live on the edge more than she was even aware. Her behavior had better not be the result of desperation on her part to find a man. Who else did she need when she had Ollie? (She was reminding herself of the obvious, not trying to be funny.) Unfortunately she wasn't paying any attention—to herself!

Speaking of Ollie, he was outside doing his business, but something about him didn't look right. Was Mira imagining as much? Then she let him in to feed him and he wouldn't eat. This was the first time he'd ever done this. She checked his crate as well as the small area (the utility room) he had access to while she was at work. Everything appeared to be intact, as in he hadn't devoured anything in the interim, which had happened on a couple occasions.

Not knowing why Ollie was ill was the worst scenario of all and not because Mira was supposed to go to Eric's in a couple hours. Admittedly, it was troubling he might not be "well" by then. Nonetheless, she decided to take a shower and "get ready" as if she was indeed going out.

Ollie didn't get worse but still looked uncomfortable. Mira tried to give him a spoonful of yogurt, but he wouldn't touch it. Even though she was dressed and ready to go to Eric's, she couldn't leave, not with Ollie looking so miserable. At the same time, she didn't want to disappoint him. Would he even believe her? It was possible he'd think she was making up an excuse not to show up because she was afraid. Maybe he ought to be afraid? She had to giggle at that.

Mira's silly thought calmed her and she called Eric. He answered immediately and she explained her predicament. If he was angry he didn't sound like it, telling her, "Take your time, Mira. See how he is in thirty or forty, even forty-five minutes and call me back. I'll keep everything on simmer from this point on and wait for your call."

Exactly forty minutes later, Mira tried again to give Ollie some yogurt, but he still wouldn't eat it. She was so frustrated she started crying—yet she wasn't sure exactly what had her so upset. Then it occurred to her she didn't want to cripple the opportunity to begin a relationship with Eric because she was overly concerned about her dog. Then again, if Eric couldn't be at least somewhat understanding....

Mira waited another five minutes and tried again to give Ollie a little yogurt—a very small spoonful this time. Albeit reluctantly he ate it. Hurray! However, she wasn't about to assume he was O.K. and she could dash off to Eric's. Ollie would still have to be monitored until bedtime. When she called Eric, she would explain the situation the best she could without sounding too "weird."

Eric's reply to Mira's call was: "If you want to take the dog to the veterinarian to be sure he's all right, I could take you. Then we could swing back over to my place and have dinner."

The invite was so forward and generous(?), at first Mira was at a loss as to what to say. Was he trying to be helpful or emotionally throw her off? Maybe she'd already been alone too long to bother being in another relationship.

Meanwhile, Mira's mother, Elisa, had been consoling her daughter by reminding her that being with a total jerk was worse than being alone. Her mother had even started taking Mira out for lunch or dinner every weekend, since Mira had broken up with her last boyfriend. Elisa had lost her husband, Earl, Mira's father, when Mira was just a toddler. Mira never had a chance to know him, or she would have gotten to find out what a good husband was. Elisa had never married again because no one could begin to compare to him.

Mira ended up telling Eric it probably wouldn't be necessary to take Ollie to the emergency veterinary clinic, but she wasn't sure, which was why she wanted to stay home and keep an eye on him.

Eric was totally cool with her decision and the reason for it. As it was, she'd explained far more than she'd intended. She liked to think she got a pretty good idea about Eric's true character following their exchange. Hopefully she was right.

In the very early morning hours, Eric had texted Mira to ask her to come over the following evening: "I'm not giving up easily Mira! LOL! I invite you to dine with me tonight (a new day!!!). PLEASE let me know ASAP. Sweet dreams. E."

Mira wasn't sure what to think, reading the text the next morning while getting ready for work. It was imperative she keep reminding herself to be on her guard. Why get involved with Eric if she was so apprehensive? She found him extremely likable yet it was so different, having him approach her out of the blue like he did. It was kind of a turn-on. In other words, how could she not like a man who was so obviously interested in her? Throw in the fact he was exceptionally good-looking.

Even though Mira had accepted Eric's second dinner invitation, she completely forgot about texting him back! Of course she still wanted to see him and had been telling herself she'd been acting ridiculous, being so suspicious of him. She was in fact glad Eric approached her in the parking lot at Goldust Crossing. She had Ollie to thank for helping her keep her head, but she still craved human companionship too.

So Mira texted Eric before leaving for work and he texted right back. They ended up texting back and forth a few times, and he made some playful comments, nothing crude or tasteless. More than ever, she couldn't wait to get to know him and spend some time with him.

Mira took care of Ollie when she got home from work, including taking him for a short walk. He wanted to go as far as the overlook, but she was anxious to start getting ready to go to Eric's. She had a feeling they would be doing more than just having dinner together, and it could turn into a longer evening than expected, not that she'd mind.

Once Mira had showered and dressed, she put on some make-up, including some heavy strokes with black liquid eye liner. Then her phone rang. It was Eric. Pleasantries quickly exchanged, he next said, "I am sorry to call you on such short notice, but I won't be able to have you over for dinner, Mira. I was so looking forward to it."

Mira's heart literally sank upon hearing that, and it was due to her counting on Eric's company. She could not let his sudden cancellation sink her into depression. In other words she was ashamed of herself. Ollie came looking for her, and she petted him while finishing her call with Eric, which consisted of telling him, "I was looking forward to it too. Anyway, thanks for calling."

He responded, "No problem. I'll call you later."

Mira ended up sitting on the floor in her bedroom, her back against the bedspread, petting Ollie and feeling very sorry for herself. It was that or go crazy, wondering if Eric just cancelled on her, to f##k with her head. She could have asked for a reason why he had to cancel, but actually she was too surprised to do so. As it was, she was too polite to do something like that anyway. She'd found herself at his mercy, perhaps intentionally on his part?

Ten-ish, Mira put Ollie in his bedtime area, and she checked her phone one last time before turning it off for the night. She'd gotten a text from Eric: "Mira, thinking about you. Sorry about tonight! Mom called and can't tell her no when she needs something! Could I pick you up at your place tomorrow about seven and take you to a favorite restaurant of mine?"

After reading the text again, Mira decided it was time to "play hard to get" and let him do some wondering. So she turned off her phone and the bedside lamp before going to sleep almost immediately.

When Mira awoke the next morning, right away she regretted not answering Eric's text last night. Playing hard to get was a horrible idea. She was anxious and the day hadn't even started, so she texted him an apology for not replying to his text sooner and told him she would see him at seven that night. Then she shamelessly gave him her address: "414 West 66th Circle." Since it was a dead-end, wasn't it safer than a through street?

Eric loved Mira, he really did. The problem was her #@*&ing dog! Eric HATED IT! Eric saw a dog and had to restrain himself from murdering the thing. In this situation there was no getting around this dog, as in it wasn't old enough to croak soon, and the thing was an integral part of Mira's life. Maybe the thing would fall over the cliff Mira liked to walk him to almost every day. As it was, dogs didn't live very long (in relative terms). He was so repelled by dogs he'd done some research on them. Even when there had been a dog in his family, he wasn't the one who took care of it. As for telling Mira he took care of his mother's dog when she went away? Wishful thinking on his part. (Never mind he'd lied.) His mother was aware of how much he hated dogs, so she used a boarding kennel whenever she went away.

Anyway, Eric was thrilled with the fact Mira was very interested in him, so he'd have to "forget" about her dog for the time being. That wasn't impossible, given how much she turned him on. She was even apologetic in a text, about having failed to respond sooner than she did to his text, inviting her to dinner someplace tonight. He'd told her he had a favorite place in mind—no such luck! Nonetheless he'd think of a restaurant that would impress her and she'd hopefully like. He'd make up a story about his family having once owned it or some other nonsense and she'd believe him! She was just gullible enough to be lovable but not annoying. She wasn't dumb but was definitely way into her dog.

9

Honest, Eric wasn't making fun of Mira. He had her address and was picking her up at seven. There was just one catch. He wouldn't be there. But he was a gentleman. He would let her know he was canceling, although it might be last-minute. And she'd buy right into it because he already had her. He wished there wasn't a damned dog practically physically attached to her.

Since Eric had Mira where he wanted her (or so he thought), it wasn't too early to put a solid plan together to get rid of the dog. However, it was imperative he not be in too big of a hurry or it would look suspicious. Patience was in order. He had plenty of that, along with intelligence, so he would get what he wanted, which was marriage. Finally maybe his mother would lay off him on that issue. Admittedly he liked the sound of being Mira's husband, although he'd spent zero time cohabitating with a girlfriend. He'd stayed over at one's place, and he'd had them spend time at his (place). That alone proved he knew how to keep his condominium clean. But he wasn't an obsessive neat-freak, so that wasn't why he hated dogs. He just HATED THEM. Was it required to provide a reason why? As far as Eric was aware, Mira didn't sleep with her dog. She'd better not or it was a possible deal-break-er, as in he couldn't wrap his head around what kind of person would want her (or his) dog (or cat) in bed with her (or him).

The first time Eric had sat and chatted with Mira was at "Coffee Haus" at Goldust Crossing. It was a couple doors down from "Doggie Suds," where she had her dog groomed. Eric had been at the strip mall to pick up a prescription at "Mountain View Market and Pharmacy" and had been getting out of his car when he spotted her walking toward the storefronts. He was crestfallen to see her enter Doggie Suds of all places. Nonetheless, he couldn't stop thinking about her not only because she looked gorgeous but the way she walked. She didn't have the assuming stride most tall, attractive women seemed to have.

MORE DOGS AND THEIR TWISTED TALES–
AND ONE CAT STORY

Here was the catch: Eric just fell in love with a woman "from a distance." Wasn't that crazy? (He was a control-freak.) He'd told himself he'd only approach her if she happened to come back out with her dog at the same time he came out of Mountain View with his prescription. And her dog had better not weigh more than fifty pounds. Anybody who lived in an urban area with a dog that weighed more than that was paranoid.

The opportunity to introduce himself to Mira was too good for Eric to pass up. She was about to put her sheared Sheltie in her white Jeep Patriot when he came up right behind her and asked to pet her beautiful dog for a minute. He purposely blew her away with his request. It helped he was really handsome if he did say so himself. Obviously he approved of her. And how could a guy who hated dogs identify a certain breed? It was interesting how hatred of something made you as curious as if you were infatuated with it— at least in his case.

Anyway, it was very flattering having Mira agree to have coffee with Eric at Coffee Haus. Naturally she brought her dog, "Ollie," because she couldn't be expected to leave him in her vehicle. Given the animal was just shaved and it wasn't that warm out, she could have left it in her Jeep. He wasn't about to hold it against her because he was way too attracted to her (lust temporarily made him forgiving).

Since Ollie was joining them, Mira and Eric had to sit outside Coffee Haus, but that was O.K. The chairs were comfy, the weather was perfect...Eric was even able to ignore her dog for the most part but did briefly pat the thing on its head once, reminding himself doing so would look good. And the dog ignored him overall, anyway. Eric just hoped Mira didn't notice. After all, couldn't dogs "smell" if a person liked dogs or had a dog? It was doubtful dogs were smart enough to read his mind, or Mira's would have already figured out Eric wanted to put a spike through its skull. Then at least Eric would finally have Mira's full attention.

11

But Eric put up a "good front," and he was extremely proud of himself for hiding how he felt. He enjoyed spending time with his recent acquaintance and couldn't wait to get to know her. He was the first to admit he could be very picky, which probably looked to the rest of the world like he was a total neurotic.

At this point Eric had to think about everything, let it sink in. Sometimes he wasn't able to appreciate a moment until it had already passed. He'd occasionally been in therapy because of this "problem." However, he didn't need therapy to figure out he wanted to see Mira again. He couldn't stop thinking about her!

Four years later, Ollie had white hair around his muzzle, where formerly it was caramel-colored. The damned dog turned out to be irresistible! Eric actually made that admission, having not only failed to "get rid of the dog," but he forgot about it, thanks to falling deeply in love with its owner.

Eric still hated the dog. But it was finally old enough, it would be dying soon, wouldn't it? It was six when Mira and he met, and now it was ten. (It just had a birthday.) Thankfully she didn't celebrate with a cake and party hats, but she did congratulate Ollie and kissed its head! Ugh!

Luckily Mira (still) had no clue Eric detested her pooch. Meanwhile, she had finally come around to the idea of having a baby with him, so he figured once he got her pregnant he could off the dog. She wouldn't care because she'd be too consumed with her pregnancy. Or so he hoped. As it was, she probably realized enough was enough, pretending to be a mom by taking care of a stupid dog.

Mira did not want to adopt, should she not be able to get pregnant "the natural way." They were trying, but it seemed like one of them wasn't very fertile. Of course Mira blamed herself and no one else, which was fine with him. In all honesty he could take or leave them having a kid, he just wanted the damned dog out of the picture. Was he sufficiently clear on that yet?

Eric just got some late-breaking news: Mira was going out of town this weekend for some sort of work-related conference. She wasn't clear on the particulars, but he didn't care because all he could think about was how he just had a golden opportunity handed to him, to take out her effing dog. It was what Eric had been waiting for all this time, as he would be in charge of taking care of Ollie. Mira didn't have the sense to board him, like his mother would do for her dog, despite the lie Eric told Mira. (And his mother's dog had since passed away, but she wasn't sure about getting another dog because her health wasn't the greatest.)

There was never a reason to suspect Mira might have a lover she met up with when taking occasional day-long excursions, so Eric didn't suspect she might be meeting someone on this trip. Usually she'd leave Ollie in the utility room when she'd be away all day whether it was because of work or something else. She never asked Eric to even check to make sure Ollie had water, let alone take him for a short walk, such as to the overlook and back. Eric always figured Mira didn't want to inconvenience him and was still getting used to being married, as in she wasn't used to having a 24/7, live-in friend and lover. But now she was obviously comfortable with the situation.

The morning of Mira's departure, she was feeling especially amorous and must have really had babies on the brain. It was possible she'd be gone as long as three nights, should she decide at the last minute to stay for some "Sunday evening classes." If that was the case, she'd drive home Monday morning. That sounded like a long way away! Hey, Eric happened to love her! She was never the problem; it was her idiotic dog. However, for the first time Eric would be alone with the dog for three days, entrusted to feed and water it as well as take it for walks.

It was so funny, Eric had yet to even take Ollie on a walk, just the two of them. He had gone with Mira and the dog a

13

few times, but that was it. What made her think her dog even wanted to walk with Eric?

It was amazing how little the person you'd been married to for four years, let you know him. Mira felt so—undercut, for want of a better word. But she wouldn't take it personally. Instead she would attempt to make sure Eric's "other side" was on display—that being his absolute hatred of Ollie if not all dogs.

After work, Eric would be taking Ollie on a walk to the overlook. Or Mira expected him to do so. He would probably try to toss Ollie over the safety barrier, and that was doing some assuming. (She was also praying it didn't actually happen.) She intended to videotape the incident, provided she could control her nerves. She wasn't going to hide once Eric tried to hurt Ollie in any way. It was a hell of a wobbly plan, but it was all she had to go on, having lived with her suspicions for years. That alone was driving her insane, hence her willingness to risk Ollie's life in the name of some solid proof. He was pretty spunky, even in his advancing years, so she fully expected him to put up a struggle, should Eric try to force him into anything.

What got Mira upset even before considering Erie's hatred of Ollie, was how she was compelled to spy on him! Was she the truly insane one? This man was the love of her life! He was totally devoted to her and treated her respectfully, all the while being hot as hell! Not only that he was great in bed! All this deserved to be mentioned because it helped keep their marriage solid. And he wasn't a slob around the house, but he wasn't a neat-freak, either. She didn't mind doing his laundry as long as he managed to throw everything in the washing machine (versus leaving it strewn on the floor).

Mira had been biding her time (for years), trying to think of a way to catch Eric being mean to Ollie in some way, but that never happened. In fact, Eric was quite friendly toward Ollie, although Eric never went out of his way to have much interaction with her dog. This way, with Mira supposedly going out of town for a couple days, Erie finally had to be 100% involved with Ollie. If Eric really did ever care for his mother's dog when she went away, he must have detested every second of it.

There they were, Eric and Ollie. They were approaching the turnaround at the overlook, walking much more slowly than Mira ever did. Ollie was always tugging on the leash, a habit she wished he'd break. Anyway, what impeccable timing on her part; she didn't want to "get in place" too early but didn't want to miss the whole thing. It couldn't have been over-emphasized, how difficult it was for Mira to go through with this, as silly as it seemed.

About thirty seconds later, Eric attempted to hurl Ollie over the wire railing, just like that! It was obvious Eric had been trying to surprise Ollie but failed. Not only that, Ollie freed himself of his collar, which Mira hadn't tightened before departing on her "business trip." And she'd assumed she thought of everything.

Anyway, Eric was left holding a leash with a collar attached to it but no dog. The image was so hilarious, Mira almost laughed. As it was, she was supposed to have been videotaping everything, but the notion of doing so had been forgotten long ago.

The upside was Ollie ran toward home (and where Mira was hiding). Meanwhile, Eric screamed, "Fine, asshole, leave! Go the hell home! I'll kill you there instead!"

Despite everything Mira had suspected, witnessed, and finally heard, she was completely undone by how gruff and downright mean Eric sounded when uttering his send-off to Ollie. Nonetheless, she'd have to face him shortly. She prefaced it by emerging from behind a creosote bush, causing Ollie to stop in his tracks. Furiously wagging his tail, he immediately tried to jump on her, which she usually scolded him about. This time, however, she hugged him. So much for teaching him manners.

15

Eric silently approached Mira and Ollie. She couldn't tell if he was repentant, so she first said, "Just throw me the collar and leash so I can walk Ollie home."

"Mira, you lied about going out of town," Eric admonished her, making her feel like a child. Never before had he used that tone of voice with her.

"I needed to create an excuse to pretend I left so I could find out the truth about you. You hate Ollie, and I taped the whole incident with you trying to throw him into the abyss."

"It's a scenic overlook, honey, or even a cliff but certainly not an abyss."

And Mira just tossed a second lie at her "beloved" husband. What of it? He was getting what he deserved. She would finish things off by divorcing him.

Mira named her baby Oliver but called him "Ollie." He was already almost five and would be starting kindergarten in a few months. It was unbelievable how quickly time went by. Her dog, Ollie, had passed away in his sleep, late last year. At least she was able to enjoy some time with him following her divorce from Eric. That was quickly finalized only because she told him he didn't have to pay child support if he hurried things along. To top it off she was very flexible with Eric's schedule for visitation with Ollie. However, she had court approval to refuse Eric's requests to take their son on any outings. When Ollie was older he could decide for himself which parent he wanted to spend the most time with. Therefore, Ollie was predominantly Mira's responsibility, and she wouldn't have had it any other way. That wasn't to say she was trying to turn her son against his father, not her.

It was time to get another dog, maybe a puppy from a shelter. Doing so would provide a great opportunity for Ollie to learn all about taking care of a canine companion. Meanwhile, Mira missed walking Ollie (the dog), especially in the evening after dinner, as it was very relaxing (yet she got some exercise). With her son getting older, he could accompany them. She never did get into pushing him in a stroller.

Out of the blue, Oliver appeared from his bedroom and announced, "Mom, I wanna like dogs too, like you."

Stepping away from the kitchen counter, where Mira was rinsing the dinner dishes, she patted the back of her son's head, saying, "I want you to too, honey, I really, really do."

If Only

Got dog? At thirty-five, Paula Milanski finally did. That was how long it took, by the time she had the income as well as a property of her own with a fenced backyard. She couldn't have a dog when she was a kid because her mother, Jane, was a neat-freak. What incensed Paula wasn't the fact she had to wait so long to have a dog but the fact she was exposed to so few germs as a child she became sick easily. Meanwhile, unbeknownst to her a powerful virus was suddenly wiping out millions, and the virus made dogs instantaneously possessed by evil spirits, should they contract the illness from their infected owners.

At forty Paula still thought about an experience at age seven, when she visited Mrs. Taylor, whose dog had a litter of six adorable black and white puppies of indeterminate breed. Paula walked to Mrs. Taylor's with her best friend, Winnie Ramero, on a cold, dreary Sunday afternoon in late March. Where Winnie and Paula lived, the semi-rural town of Brewster, Indiana, there were sidewalks. However, Mrs. Taylor's place was outside the town limits and was in fact quite a distance. Nonetheless the two girls had visited the elderly lady on quite a few occasions. She had a rambling old house on a couple acres with a dilapidated barn in the back. Winnie was allowed to visit Mrs. Taylor because she was "a friend of the family," and that made it O.K. for Paula to accompany her.

It killed Paula, her mother hardly gave a shit what her daughter was up to, but her mother's antennae went straight up when Paula would return home from Mrs. Taylor's with mud on her shoes. It seemed like the weather was always inclement when Winnie and Paula went to see her.

On this occasion, Winnie had been given the go-ahead to "pick out a puppy" and could bring him or her home after he or she was weaned. After a mere couple minutes, Winnie made her choice, which amazed Paula. She would have had to think about it for a day or two. That didn't matter because Paula was never going to have the opportunity to pick out a puppy. Not only were they too germ-ridden, they weren't free. Paula noticed Winnie handing Mrs. Taylor a fifty dollar bill. Paula's mother never would have trusted her daughter with that much money for anything.

With Paula's mother having passed away recently, Paula had to wonder if she was the only child who didn't cry upon a parent's death? Undoubtedly not. Paula was sad about her passing, but she'd get over it. One thing Paula learned, having been raised by a hardworking single mom, it was imperative she be "tough" and "stand up for herself." That helped give Paula the impetus to move to Scottsdale, Arizona, 100% to get away from her suffocating former life.

Paula's mother was super-controlling, even when dead! Paula didn't blame her mother, she blamed herself. Her mother could have gotten a dog, which would have given her something to worry about besides her daughter. Paula wasn't trying to bring the subject back to Mrs. Taylor and her puppies but why not. That day, Paula had wanted to get a puppy because Winnie was getting one. Paula would have preferred a solid brown or black dog. At her age then, she didn't mentally go much further than picking a favorite color for a dog.

Since Paula was at work from seven to four, Monday through Friday, her first criteria for a dog was "one with patience." She figured the best way to meet that goal was adopt an older shelter dog. Besides, it seemed like the hardest dog to be adopted. She'd educated herself somewhat about dogs and was aware they didn't live nearly as long as humans. Nonetheless, getting one that was six or seven would still have several years left, at least she expected as much. Holding her own fluffy little puppy would have to wait.

"Robbie" was 12 to Paula's forty. He had coarse black fur and weighed about thirty-five pounds. "Short and stout" best described him, as he had stubby legs and a rather long body but was big-boned. His nose was long and he had expressive brown eyes as well as black tufts of hair above them, like 3-D eyebrows, adding to his cuteness. Even in his golden years Robbie was cute.

Naturally Paula's mother never gave Paula any credit for the fact her daughter was financially independent. In other words: THERE WAS NO MAN IN THE PICTURE. Was Mom satisfied? Even though Jane didn't think there was a man "good enough" for her daughter, Paula herself was never "good enough" for her mother!

"Come in, Robbie," Paula told her dog, having let him out after she got home from work. He had been enjoying the phenomenal fall weather. Usually it was blistering hot this time of the year and then the bottom fell out. December would have mornings that were barely above freezing. Even though Robbie didn't know the backyard of Paula's house was artfully landscaped, she'd expected her mother would notice when Paula had invited her to visit shortly after buying the property. The previous owner had been a landscape designer and obviously also enjoyed his career as a pastime. Fortunately the man had a dog, so he'd made sure to include a grassy area.

It was Friday night and yet again Paula didn't have a date. However, that didn't bother her because she'd been "dateless" for so long she considered herself "undesirable." Her mother would be thrilled, were she still alive. By the way, when she (Jane) had made that initial visit to Paula's new home, having flown to Phoenix from Indianapolis, she'd made so many negative comments, Paula vowed to never invite her back again (and didn't). Fortunately, her mother had made a reservation to stay at the Ritz-Carlton, so she couldn't also be a griping houseguest.

One remark Paula's mother made, really stuck with Paula, when referring to the backyard: "What a mess. All that vegetation is going to get out of hand if you don't keep ahead of it, which I doubt you will since you never owned a house before."

And Paula never "owned" a dog before, yet she liked to think she'd managed to take pretty decent care of Robbie. Paula almost wished her mother would have stepped in a pile of dog shit that Paula might have missed picking up that day, but it would have ended up in her house, most likely. No one paid less attention to the cleanliness of other houses than her mother. In other words, once Jane Milanski left home she became a slob.

If only Paula had seen right through her mother's hypocrisy all along, she could have called her out on it, and they could have had a smoother relationship than they did. (Paula was willing to take no more than minimal responsibility for them not getting along.)

The (mobile) phone rang, jostling Paula awake, not that she was asleep per se. She'd been watching TV with Robbie at her feet and had been "relaxing." She didn't know what program was on because there was a commercial on the channel. At work she was on her feet a lot, so of course she was tired upon returning home. However, she always first took Robbie on a walk. As they'd both aged, the walks had become more brief. Paula was too lazy to push herself, and lately she'd noticed her weight creeping up. Getting fat from "old age" sounded depressing! It was bad enough she'd never married nor had any kids. She didn't have a lot confidence as it was, so becoming a fat old cow would seal her fate for sure: she would enter her "golden years" having never done more than go on a handful of dates with a couple of men. At this point she was happy her dog liked her, at least.

"Paula, it's Jack, from work," he said. She couldn't

21

believe it. Was there a problem? The last notion she'd ever have was he'd called to talk to her and/or ask her out.

But he did ask her out, just like that. For tonight! It was already 6:30, so it was already "night" as far as Paula was concerned. Nonetheless, she agreed without a moment's hesitation, shocking herself. However, Jack didn't sound surprised at all, although he did say, "Great." Was he aware she'd had her eye on him since the day she started working at "Personalization Station," a company specializing in personalized embroidered clothing and other promotional items? He might not have been every woman's idea of handsome, but he certainly was for her.

Robbie wouldn't even notice Paula was gone for a couple hours. She'd take him for his usual "last break" when she got home. There would be a self-imposed curfew because the last thing Paula wanted to do was seem like she was "easy" or only wanted a one-night stand. Having a long-term relationship with a man continued to be her "goal" but she also needed to be O.K. with the possibility she might indeed remain single her whole life. Still, she couldn't wait to get ready to go out tonight. If only she had something to wear that had a "wow factor." Obviously it was impossible to go shopping first, so she'd have to use her imagination, using what was in her closet. Unfortunately she was "too fat" for any jeans or pants that might have passed for "sexy." Then again, she was 40. Who was she trying to fool?

Granted, Jack was close to the same age as her, or she was pretty sure he was. At least he wasn't after a "young hottie." How could she compete with one of those, even if she lost weight?

Rather than bore anyone with the details of "the date," Paula preferred to just say she was thrilled to get home and take Robbie out. And he was so happy to see her he must have noticed after all, she'd left.

Jack was nice and all that, but he made practically no

effort to start any sort of conversation with her. Since Paula needed a distraction and was starving, she ate like a pig. It was probably a huge turn-off for Jack, but he didn't exactly drive her crazy with desire. She wanted to say she was glad she wouldn't have to see him again, but he'd be at work tomorrow, just like her. It was highly unlikely he'd ask her out again, which would be doing her a favor. In other words, he didn't have to be concerned about any "pressure." Paula was relieved the pressure was off her to fit into any "sexy" jeans.

The morning after "the date," Paula awoke with a terrible stomach ache. It felt like whatever she'd eaten last night was trying to drill its way out of her stomach. Maybe it was still too soon for last evening's meal to be doing damage to her digestive system, but why not blame "the date" on it, since the date itself was so lousy?

Paula felt another pang in her stomach and rolled over, hoping to make it disappear. Instead, doing so made matters worse. She had to feel better than this, or she wouldn't be able to go to work. The shrimp in the shrimp cocktail must have done this. Jack was the one who'd ordered it. If something she ate a day earlier was the real culprit, Paula was determined to blame the shrimp because she hardly ever ate seafood—specifically because she was paranoid something like this would happen.

Jack had insisted Paula try some of his appetizer, despite her telling him she didn't want any—more than once. Nevertheless, she ate some, if only to "be polite." As dumb as that sounded, it wasn't surprising that was her reasoning. Was it possible Paula had some sort of allergic reaction to the seafood? "Why not?" was the natural response. It all went back to her mother, who never exposed her to enough germs, starting with letting her have a puppy—but, as mentioned, not especially one of Mrs. Taylor's. Also, if she'd had a puppy as a child, she might not have ended up being so neurotic.

Moreover, without her health, all else was irrelevant.

Here was Robbie, who needed to go out. "Just a minute," Paula told him, suddenly unable to move. That was the last thing she "felt."

Jack had the distinct "pleasure" of doing a well-being check on Paula Milanski! Yesterday he was jokingly told to check on her, as she hadn't shown up for work and wouldn't answer her phone (or reply to any texts). There were winks and smiles in Jack's direction all day, and he didn't bother pointing out he never even kissed her on the cheek, let alone spent the night with her. By late morning of day two of Paula's absence, there was suddenly widespread concern. After all, Paula was an employee with a perfect attendance record, something Jack could not lay claim to.

Toward the end of the work day, Jack's boss, Jered Smalls, approached him and said, "I'm outta here. I'm head-ed for the driving range to hit some balls before the wife gets home. She'll get home the same time as me and think I worked as long as she did! Anyway, enough of my personal life. Lemme know what you find out after you go to Paula's, O.K.? I like that girl. I hope she's all right."

Jack nodded his acknowledgement of what his boss said but was thinking about the fact he wished he'd never asked Paula out. It turned out to be a boring date, but that was his fault as much as hers. He happened to like her a lot, but it probably seemed like he was at best indifferent. Truthfully, spending time with her one-on-one made him so "in awe of her," he was practically speechless for the duration of the date.

Hopefully Paula was O.K. and didn't fall in the shower, breaking her leg (or worse). The talk at work was she had no family, other than a "Mrs. Taylor," who wasn't even a blood relative. Paula was raised by her mother, who'd passed away, although Jack wasn't sure how long ago. Paula's dog consti-tuted her family, how sad was that? Then again, Jack moved to the Phoenix area to get away from his parents and two sisters, all of whom still lived in Tucson. Still, he wasn't as far from them as Paula was from her mother, who'd remained in the Midwest when her daughter made the long trek out here.

So Paula and Jack not only both liked dogs but were kind of loners, at least when it came to getting away from their families. However, it was comforting for Jack to know his family was only an hour and a half away, even less if you liked to speed.

Jack reached Paula's one-story, tan stucco house with an attached one-and-a-half car garage. Her car must have been in there, as there wasn't a vehicle in the driveway. Nonetheless, he parked in the street! Why hadn't he pulled into the driveway?

As Jack was exiting his white Ford Escape, he heard a dog bark from inside Paula's house. What was her dog's name? Bobbie? Robbie? Yeah, Robbie. Jack should have asked Paula about her dog, giving them something to talk about. Maybe once he located her (and hopefully she was O.K.) he could ask her out again and "make the date up to her."

The terra-cotta-colored front door was ajar. No wonder her dog's bark had sounded so loud! Paula had to be home if she left the door open like that.

Jered Smalls glanced at his watch after playing nine holes of golf at a cow pasture of a course. He'd intended to only hit some balls, but the course was so empty he couldn't resist. Now he would be later getting home than he'd anticipated, but that was all right; his wife, Melissa, would still be told he had to work late. No matter what she always believed him! (And he loved her all the more because of as much.)

After putting his clubs in his red Corvette Z06, Jered called Jack Naylor. The guy was supposed to have contacted him regarding Paula Milanski. In this case was "no news" possibly "good news?" In other words did the two fall into each other's arms upon Naylor's arrival at Paula Milanski's? As much as Jered wanted to believe that possibility, he remained skeptical.

Fortunately Jered had a file folder he kept with him at all times, containing addresses and contact information for all his employees. The first order of business was to call Naylor. If he didn't answer, he'd try calling Paula, although he'd already tried to do that several times. He probably should call 9-1-1 by this point, but since he'd waited this long, regarding Paula Milanski, a few more minutes wouldn't make a difference, would it?

Of course Naylor didn't answer his phone, so after looking up Paula Milanski's address, Jered headed to her house. It was actually kind of on his way home, anyway. Before leaving the Desert Oasis Public Golf Club, Jered called Melissa and told her he was just leaving work. He smiled afterward, smugly thinking about how she once again believed him.

Jered reached Hermosa Avenue, which was wide, flat and palm tree-lined, with small but well-maintained one-story brick and stucco homes on either side. Some had significantly more southwestern accents than others. Paula Milanski's was the latter, and it also had a wide concrete driveway leading to a one-and-a-half car garage. Most of the houses on the street had carports.

All that and Naylor's Ford Escape was parked in the street? Jered had no intention of leaving his Corvette on Hermosa Avenue, even though he only intended to be here a few minutes.

The first thing Jered noticed when approaching the front door was it was ajar. Assuming the two lovers were in there "being intimate," why the hell would they be so careless? Then again, in comparative terms, they were "young and dumb." Jered didn't think a lot of Naylor, but he liked Paula Milanski. Maybe he just felt sorry for her because it was said she lived alone and had no family in the area—or maybe no family at all, he wasn't sure.

MORE DOGS AND THEIR TWISTED TALES–
AND ONE CAT STORY

What Jered had expected to do was knock on the front door and be told, "Just a minute," by either Paula or Jack from somewhere within the house. Eventually one of them would open the door. Since that scenario wouldn't be playing out, Jered had to make a new plan.

Jered decided to knock on the slightly-opened door, saying, "Paula, are you home?" Hearing nothing, he decided to go inside. As he was about to shut the door behind him, he called Naylor (by his first name, Jack). That was when Jered heard a dog growl ominously. He reached for the door handle so he could leave, but the house was dark and he was too late.

It only looked like Paula Milanski was having a party at her house. That would have been the day, given what a spinster-loner she was. Patty Lerner knew more about the goings on Hermosa Avenue than anyone else because she not only had a two-year-old daughter to babysit but home schooled her seven-year-old son. If she could get the two kids to take a nap at the same time, Patty used some of that "free time" to sit and stare out the living room window, just like a dog. Paula's house was directly across the street from Patty and her husband Kenneth's place. (Patty was determined their house was nicer even though it had the same floor plan as Paula's.)

Kenneth always told Patty she was "too nosy for her own good," but she considered herself curious and nothing more. There was no harm in that, was there? He also said she wasn't busy enough, but he was clueless as to how much effort went into her days, taking care of two kids. Whenever he mentioned they should have one more, she rolled her eyes. Obviously the financial aspect of a third child wasn't a burden to him. Then again, he traveled a lot for work and never seemed to tire of it. The rewarding salary was an ongoing incentive, most likely.

Patty happened to be looking out the floor-to-ceiling living room window right at this moment, preferring the carpeted floor to a chair. Also, her kids were still napping. Obviously the other residents on the street were in a coma, as no one had called the police about the vehicles parked at Paula's for the past two days—some in the street and two in the driveway. So Patty called 9-1-1 and waited.

It didn't take long for a squad car to arrive as well as an ambulance shortly thereafter. The vehicles were maneuvered so as not to block the street. However, moments later a fire truck appeared and planted itself right in the middle of the street, also partially blocking the driveway of Patty's house.

Then Mr. Moore showed up in his brand-new, white Dodge minivan. He actually attempted to drive around the fire truck before giving up and pulling into Patty's driveway. Patty was too busy watching him and his minivan to pay any attention to what was going on across the street, although some of her view was obstructed by the fire truck. Another squad car appeared and parked behind the fire truck. Now Mr. Moore's minivan was stuck indefinitely in Patty's driveway.

Patty would step outside and ask Mr. Moore if he'd like to wait in the house. Being elderly, he should have been the epitome of patience, but there was no need to make him sit in his minivan. He could always walk home, but he lived pretty far down the street and had a discernible limp.

Before leaving the house, Patty listened to make sure her kids still weren't stirring. Then she put on her shoes and unlocked the front door on her way out, as she didn't have a key with her. Given the numerous vehicles that were parked on the street, it was nonetheless strange how quiet it was outside.

Patty and Mr. Moore greeted one another and she asked him, "Would you care to wait in the house until the emergency vehicles get out of the street?"

"I'm all right for the time being, but I would like to know exactly what the commotion's about. Who lives in the house right across the street from you?"

"Paula Milanski."

"Who?"

"Paula Milanski," Patty repeated. "She lives there alone... with her dog. She takes him for short walks and that's about the only time she leaves the house. She goes to work too, though. I finally called nine-one-one because there were vehicles parking in front of her house and even in the driveway, and they never left. It was beyond strange in my opinion, and I knew no one else on the street was going to do anything about it."

Mr. Moore said, "I vote we go over there ourselves and maybe we can see something from the front yard."

"I can't leave my kids," Patty told him. "I unlocked the front door and don't even have a key with me. They've got to be waking up from their naps by this time for sure."

Mr. Moore said, "I think I'll head over there myself and take a gander, if the cops and emergency people will even let me get close. Maybe I can at least find out what the heck's going on."

"That sounds good," Patty said. "Maybe you could stop back at the house afterward and let me know what you found out. I'll be here with my kids."

"Okee-doke," Mr. Moore said as he exited his van. After a quick wave he turned and limped down the driveway and crossed the street, soon disappearing behind the massive fire truck parked in the middle of the street.

Patty went inside and became caught up with her kids, who'd long ago awakened from their naps. The eldest had taken the milk from the refrigerator and tried to drink it straight from the gallon jug. Fortunately it was almost empty, or more would have spilled than it did when it was dropped on the gray tile floor.

It was impossible for Patty not to be proud of herself for quickly getting things returned to normal. However, after plenty of time had passed, Mr. Moore should have returned from doing his "investigation" across the street. Maybe he purposely hadn't because she'd sounded like she'd ordered him to do so. Some old people had that kind of attitude (and she didn't blame them). He might have simply forgotten and went home to wait until it was time to retrieve his minivan. He was probably married, so his wife could bring him back; Patty wasn't going to concern herself with the issue at this point. Nonetheless, when Kenneth came home from work—provided he could get to the house with his car—he would not be pleased to see a minivan partially blocking "his" side of the garage. Kenneth was actually a pretty easygoing individual, but some things had to be just so, especially after a long day at work. He was due to go out of town in a couple days, so he expected to come home and relax.

Again, there was no use in worrying about any of this because it was completely beyond Patty's control! Nonetheless there was one last option: provided all the emergency vehicles finally left, she could drive down to Mr. Moore's and pick him up in her minivan. His (and his wife's) house was similar to Patty and her husband's, except there was more landscaping in front, including various shrubs and flowering plants lining the concrete driveway as well as the red brick walkway leading to the front door. Evidently the Moores liked to spend a lot of time taking care of the landscaping around their house. Once Patty's kids were grown and gone, she wanted nothing more than to find a hobby, even if it was just spending more time in the yard, planting flowers. Sometimes it felt like she'd thrown her whole life away so she could be a stay-at-home wife and mother (and home-schooler). If only she hadn't become so consumed with her roles! Dedicated and conscientious to a fault, if she did say so herself.

What a day at work. What a time getting home. Traffic was snarled everywhere Kenneth went. In some instances it looked like people had literally abandoned their vehicles.

MORE DOGS AND THEIR TWISTED TALES–
AND ONE CAT STORY

Very strange. When he got to the end of Hermosa Avenue, where he lived with his wife and two kids, he was forced to park at the end of the street because it was littered with parked vehicles. When he'd left for work this morning, there had only been a couple vehicles in front of the house across the street from his and his wife's, which was Paula Milanski's. Kenneth was in fact very concerned about her. It was especially troubling seeing a number of emergency vehicles taking up much of the street in front of her house. She was about the only resident on the street who had a dog, versus a kid or two.

First things first. Kenneth would check in with his wife, Patty, and have dinner before investigating what was going on at Miss Milanski's. If only his wife was a better cook, he could actually look forward to eating dinner, versus just eating to fill his stomach.

Finally noticing a new-looking white minivan in the driveway of his and his wife's house, Kenneth thought maybe they had company. Maybe that meant Patty put more effort into making the meal delicious.

If only.

Cat Woman

Lennie hated cats until meeting the woman of his dreams. That explained the decor in his cozy man cave, in a corner of his basement. The black leather sofa facing the TV had a colorful, cat-themed throw on part of it, and there were cat-themed embroidered pillows wedged in each corner. (The pillows were purchased from a mail order catalog, already finished.) There was a cartoonish watercolor painting of a purple cat on the wall behind the sofa, and there were several cat-themed pictures on the oak-paneled walls. The small refrigerator in the corner had cat-themed magnets all over the front of it. Lennie had owned his house for a dozen years before getting around to finishing this alcove in the otherwise unfinished basement. Then he met Kit, and he didn't want to hide down here. He wanted to spend every waking moment with her, he loved her so much. She was more than welcome to cozy up with him in his man cave (the ultimate compliment), but she preferred to remain upstairs. That didn't seem strange, especially as timed passed and Lennie's eyes were opened to some really strange "habits" of Kit's. Still, he loved her. It remained unbelievable how he lost her.

What Lennie should have done was get to know Kit better before enthusiastically inviting her to live with him. It wasn't as if she'd hinted she needed a place to live or wanted to mooch off him. They'd dated for a few months, and it was taking forever to get to know her. He figured if they lived together he'd have that opportunity.

Kit was renting a townhouse in Carefree (Arizona) and

had been doing so month-to-month lately because she was looking for a place of her own. She claimed to have held off buying a house because she wasn't sure she wanted the responsibility, and it had nothing to do with having the financial capability.

The cat's name was "Theodore." That was to say, Kit's cat's name was Theodore, and Lennie had no idea she had a cat until after Kit had finally accepted the invite to move in with him. At first he was incredulous when she'd asked, "Is it O.K. if I bring my cat along?" What was he supposed to say in response? He would have killed their relationship right then if he'd told her "no."

So Lennie patiently waited for Kit to appear and move in with him. The place she was renting wasn't more than fifteen minutes away, as he lived on the north side of Scottsdale. When she did show up in a white Kia Soul, he'd expected her to emerge from it with a cat carrier in hand. Instead, she practically leaped from her vehicle, solo, wearing a long, sleek black raincoat. Lennie shamelessly stared, wondering what this enigmatic woman was up to. It was late February and kind of cool in the early evenings, but she was still a bit overdressed. Kit proceeded to throw herself at Lennie, who found himself carrying her into the house (and also found out she was naked underneath the raincoat). If this was her night to put Lennie under her spell, it worked.

The next morning a panel truck arrived with Kit's "things." Most of it was for her dear Theodore. He had his own brass bed! It was to scale for a twelve-pound cat, but still. He also had a huge, tan-carpeted play/scratch post, as well as a smaller, white-carpeted one! Was there enough room on the main level of the one-story house for all this?

See? Lennie had already accepted the fact "The Cat" was moving in too. Kit was right to give him that night to remember—so he'd conveniently "forget" about everything else.

It was possible Kit had been playing him, but it turned

out she did have the finances for a place of her own. What more proof did Lennie need once she'd offered to pay his mortgage as well as the utilities and groceries? He told her he'd take care of the mortgage, but if she wanted to help out with the rest, fine. (He was more relieved to have her financial help than he'd ever admit—to her.) As it was, it was evident from the get-go, Kit was a very private individual. Lennie respected as much and found "the mystery" about her a turn-on. She obviously had some money, and he figured more about her would be revealed as time passed.

Other than keeping the house immaculate, Kit did not have a job. It made Lennie wonder exactly how much money she must have inherited (and exactly who passed away). Why not also wonder if perhaps Kit was married before and her husband passed away under suspicious circumstances, yet she still received a payout from his life insurance policy that named her as the beneficiary?

Kit was an excellent cook. It could have been argued she had so much time on her hands, the least she could do was make sure Lennie had a delicious meal to enjoy every evening after work. However, he didn't see the situation like that at all and simply liked knowing someone was waiting for him to get home at the end of the day. It wasn't like he was lonely before, but life was definitely much better with Kit in it.

Ironically, Lennie completed the carpentry portion of his man cave (no cat-themed decorating) literally one day before "meeting" Kit. (The quote marks were there because it was strange how they'd met.) About 11:00 A.M. on a Thursday in mid-May, Lennie was doing some weeding by the front of his one-acre property. He'd had the whole week off and rather than take a trip, he'd stayed home to do this and that, including plenty of yard work. Even residences in a desert climate required plenty of maintenance. The weird part was Kit approached him from behind, as in she had been inside the property, which was surrounded on three sides by a

seven-foot cement block wall. She could have made her
entrance via the front, where the wall was only a couple feet
high (and made of red brick, versus cement block). That was
entirely plausible, especially if she snuck in before he'd come
out here to work. However, that meant she'd been hiding
somewhere on the property, most likely in some shrubs.
Crazy.

Anyway, Kit had walked up and said "hello" from behind
Lennie, startling the hell out of him. (Actually she scared him
even more than that, but he didn't want to print the word for
how startled he was.) Nonetheless, he couldn't be angry with
her for technically trespassing.

Lennie ended up greeting Kit by asking, "Can I help you?"
when he should have been admonishing her for trespassing
(he refused to give her the satisfaction of being told she
scared the shit out of him). As much as he wanted to be
angry with her, it was easier to marvel at how pretty she
looked when she smiled—which was her reply to his question. Then she stuck out her hand and introduced herself as
"Kit Matteson."

It was impossible for Lennie not to look at Kit's right
hand before shaking it, and he was struck by how long her
fingers were. The nails were long as well but were without
colored polish, which he found unusual.

Anyway, Kit was very sweet and extremely easy to talk to.
Lennie had no idea what exactly they talked about for a few
minutes, but he found himself more and more drawn to her,
almost as if she'd cast a spell. He'd never before been "in
love," so maybe that was what it was. The next thing he knew
he'd asked her out for lunch, yet there was no explanation as
to why she'd been on his property.

What was there not to like about a cat named Theodore?
That was what Lennie repeatedly told himself when he and
Kit were in bed, making love. The cat actually sat and
watched them from the ledge on the bay window. (The master

bedroom in his house had a bay window, which looked upon his walled "backyard," which had a pool—hence the wall around it as well as around the entire property.) The plantation shutters were closed while Kit and Lennie were "going at it," so it wasn't as if he wanted anyone watching them, including a cat. He never dared bringing up his opinion of Theodore "observing them," because he was certain Kit would tell him he was overreacting. After all it was "just" a cat. Looking back he wasn't so sure.

Even though Lennie had fallen in love with Kit at first sight—or he thought he did—it didn't completely blind him to Kit's "habits." And it seemed like she became comfortable with him pretty quickly, so she wasn't exactly careful to hide those "habits." Who could say for sure, but maybe she secretly wanted to give herself away, as she could never even begin to explain herself.

It wasn't long before Lennie and Kit settled into a daily routine—Lennie would go to work and Kit would spend the day mostly at home, cleaning as well as doing all the yard work. That was O.K. He didn't miss it anyway. She'd leave to run errands or have a manicure. She was obsessed with the latter, and the fact she only liked "clear-colored" polish wasn't exactly weird but was a bit peculiar.

Friday was typically a day Lennie got off work a few minutes earlier than he did, Monday to Thursday. However, on this first day of August, he got off an entire hour early. That was definitely unprecedented. Almost as unprecedented, he was going home and swim! Lennie didn't swim as much as he would have liked, especially in the summer months. Since he didn't have any yard work duties anymore, he needed a form of exercise.

The swimming pool water might be warmer than bath water, but Lennie could add some cold water from a garden hose. If it still felt hot afterward, he'd jump in anyway. One person who wouldn't join him no matter what was Kit. She always had an excuse at the ready, such as: "I just washed

my hair."Another one was: "I don't want to have to take a
shower again, just to wash off the chlorine." If she couldn't
swim or was afraid of water, Lennie wanted her to simply
admit it. He couldn't figure out why that bothered him so
much but it did. Maybe it had to do with the fact she was
such an enigma anyway. He was positive she never swam
while he was at work, so what exactly was going on? It was
tempting to throw her in the pool, to see if she could swim,
but he didn't want her to panic, in case she couldn't swim at
all and had some sort of phobia about water, as well. She'd
never forgive him, and that, he couldn't live with.

It was obvious Kit had no idea Lennie had returned
home, as she was by the pool, apparently asleep. She would
have otherwise leaped up and come inside to greet him. Her
friendliness was not only contagious, how could you not like
that kind of person? He was in the bedroom, where he'd
grabbed his swim trunks from a shelf in the walk-in closet.
Standing in front of the bay window he was changing his
clothes, as he couldn't help admiring how hot Kit looked, laying on her side, her torso slightly curled. While Lennie's swim
trunks were still around his ankles, he proceeded to nearly
fall on his ass upon witnessing Kit suddenly lift her right leg
as if she were stretching. Then she started to lick her leg!
Initially Lennie was turned on by what he was seeing until
realizing she was in fact "grooming" herself, just like a cat!

Somehow Lennie got his swim trunks up where they
belonged, and Kit continued to "groom" her right leg. The
more he witnessed of this spectacle, the more creeped-out he
became, and he was no longer turned-on. It was time for a
cold beer—or two—before he went out to the pool. Maybe he
could make his appearance "between leg-groomings."

The second Lennie turned around he was making eye
contact with none other than Kit's dear cat, Theodore. It had
evidently been sitting right behind Lennie for who knew how
long. He wanted to kick the thing in the head because it
looked like it was furious with him. A cat! It was impossible

the stupid thing had any such emotion. As it was, Kit was Lennie's girlfriend. Hello! Two humans! Lennie had priority. The cat had gotten on Lennie's nerves with its staring, as it was.

Beer in hand (the can was half-empty), Lennie returned to the bedroom bay window before going outside. He was in less and less of a hurry to do so.

Theodore had temporarily disappeared, but the most important part was the cat wasn't on the bed. Otherwise Lennie would have removed it. Although the cat didn't sleep with him and Kit, the animal liked to nap there during the day. Thankfully at least the bed had a bedspread on it, which Kit removed at bedtime. Even better, she had zero inclination to let Theodore share the bed with them.

Finally Lennie dared to look out the bay window, only to see Kit's head turned way around, not 180 degrees but close. She was licking her right shoulder—behind her, not the shoulder itself. Then she suddenly stopped and looked around, as if she'd heard something. Yeah! Her boyfriend inwardly shrieking in disbelief.

It took drinking two cans of beer before Lennie had the fortitude to surprise Kit—and he didn't intend to actually do that anyway. Instead he flung open the French doors in the kitchen and yelled, "Hello, Kit! I'm home early. I thought I'd go swimming." The whole time he'd covered his eyes, not wanting to see Kit tumble out of the chaise longue because she was indeed surprised. Not to be selfish, but at this point Lennie was more worried about himself.

In response Kit exclaimed, "Hi, honey. I'm just sunning myself for a few minutes before coming inside to start making something for dinner. Or maybe you want to go out tonight?"

"No, I'm O.K. with just hanging out at home, if you don't mind," Lennie told her. Meanwhile he couldn't help thinking about the fact she'd been by the pool for a few minutes just since he returned from work. Maybe she got so relaxed she lost track of time. He'd give her the benefit of the doubt, if only because she looked so hot in her bikini. It made it easy to forget about how strange she might be.

Lennie proceeded to have an enjoyable swim, while Kit remained on the chaise longue. Every time he'd look up from swimming, it was extremely arousing to have a view of her. Thankfully she didn't groom herself anymore, and Lennie was all too ready to pretend he imagined witnessing her doing anything weird, earlier. He hadn't been getting as much sleep lately (in part because of plenty of late night love-making), but he wasn't complaining.

While Lennie was finishing his swim by floating on his back (and was immensely proud of this "feat"), Kit must have gone in the house. He realized as much when he finally quit floating, unable to help but wonder just how impressed Kit might be with him. (By this time he couldn't have cared less if Kit did groom herself like a cat.)

After drying off, Lennie padded toward the French doors leading to the kitchen. Once he was near, he heard Kit talking. Her voice was comically sing-songy, as if she were speaking to a small child. Perhaps she was on the phone with her friend Caitlin, who in fact had a three-year-old daughter, Brianne. As much as Kit liked to spend time with those two, she had yet to even remotely act like she wanted a kid of her own. In her late twenties (at most) Kit had plenty of time to decide, but it was nonetheless interesting how detached she was about the issue.

As it turned out Kit wasn't on the phone. Lennie found that out upon peering around the corner of one of the French doors, feeling like a snoop—outside his own house! She was talking to Theodore. It wasn't unheard of for her to talk to the cat, sounding drippy-sweet, but on this occasion she was really overdoing it. Lennie couldn't decide if he was weirded out or extremely jealous. Maybe too many strange things had been happening at once, was all.

Since it was such a nice day for swimming, Lennie decided to jump back in the pool. He might even swim until dinner time.

If Lennie had momentarily considered Kit was too strange for him, he resolved to squelch any urge to believe that, thanks to the extremely passionate night they proceeded to spend together. If Kit was perpetually going overboard seducing him, all so he would "forget things," it was working. He just wished he wasn't so exhausted after yet another sexual marathon—despite also getting a decent night's sleep. Fortunately it was Saturday, so he had until Monday to rest up, provided Kit "let him." How could any man say "no" to a woman as hot and sexed up as Kit? Lennie wanted nothing more than to keep up!

Kit was known to sleep in on Saturdays, right along with him, but she did eventually get up to make breakfast, which was more elaborate than just buttered toast.

Having awakened about nine, Lennie initially felt ready to get up. Since Kit was already up and gone, there'd be no A.M. lovemaking. That was honestly a relief, as he needed to recover from the night before. Lennie decided to "close his eyes" for a couple more minutes and ended up going back to sleep. He had dream after dream, all with him a kid again, back in southern Michigan, where he grew up on an apple orchard. There was always something he was supposed to be doing, especially in the summer, but he was always so lazy! At the time he'd considered himself a daydreamer.

It was almost noon before Lennie woke back up, abruptly sitting up this time. Once the shock wore off that he'd slept too long, he wondered why Kit didn't rouse him, earlier. Did he really look that peaceful? Then he looked over at the bay window, and Theodore was sitting on the ledge, doing what else but staring (at him). Who was the real boss around here? His next question: Where was the biggest pair of shoes he owned, so he could take one and throw it at Theodore? Lennie just wanted to let the cat know what he thought of it, not injure it. Plainly Kit loved the cat, and if that was her thing, he wasn't about to scoff at her. And he expected Kit to be as open-minded toward him.

Not one morsel of a cooked meal was left for Lennie in the kitchen, so Kit had evidently washed any breakfast dishes. It was understandable since it was already lunchtime, but still. Hopefully Kit was out picking up something to eat, as there wasn't a whole lot of stuff in the refrigerator. And yes, now that Lennie had "a cook," he was more disinclined than ever to do any cooking.

Just as Lennie was about to look in the garage and (hopefully) confirm Kit's Kia wasn't in there, he found himself looking out the French doors—and there was Kit once again on the chaise longue. She was on her back this time, but at least she looked "normal," as in she was wearing a hat and sunglasses while "sunning herself," sparing her beautiful face from the ravages of the sun. Not to be shallow, but Lennie wanted this relationship to last, and he couldn't guarantee he'd be as attracted to Kit if her face was wrinkled. However, he really did love her and just needed more time before proposing (but would hurry up if she threatened to leave him). His biggest worry was she would get tired of him long before he tired of her (and he never would at this rate because he was still trying to figure out what the hell she was really about).

What was Lennie going to do this time, to get Kit's attention? Obviously he couldn't fling open the French doors and tell her he was home. Duh. He decided to take a shower and get dressed. If she was still sunning herself when he was finished, he'd go out and pick up something to eat.

O.K. Lennie was ready to go out. One last check on Kit, and she was indeed still sunning herself. What was it with her? Sure Lennie knew what laziness was, given how he was as a kid, but he liked to think he "outgrew" it as an adult. Was she stuck in arrested development or something? Obviously he had little patience for the obvious: inertness! As much as Lennie wanted to believe their relationship could last "forever," it was an unrealistic expectation.

The next thing Lennie knew, Kit leaped up, almost losing her hat. After securing it, she approached the French doors, her walk very purposeful. All Lennie could think was he'd just gotten caught ogling her, and she was about to slap him across the face and call him a pervert. He'd be devastated.

Instead Kit came inside, grabbed Lennie's hand and pulled him toward the bedroom. He was starving and honestly was not "in the mood"! Not to be graphic, but he was starting to think he was dealing with a nymphomaniac. Of course he wasn't going to fight her off so he could run to the "Jack-in-a-Box" drive-through.

Lennie did not have to be dragged to the bedroom, so it wasn't like he went there against his will. Afterward he was more hungry than ever. Kit told him she'd make something but wanted to take a shower first. He put on a pair of jeans, no shirt or shoes, and plopped down at the kitchen table with a cold beer. He hated to look like he expected to be waited on, but he was too famished to care. The only one in the household who might have a problem with Lennie sitting here relaxing, was Theodore. The cat had yet to emerge from the bedroom, where it had yet again "watched" Kit and Lennie make love. Lennie was proud of himself for holding his tongue once again about what he thought of that cat.

Suddenly Lennie heard Kit say from the bedroom, "You can't just run off forever! We need to discuss this more first! Remember, I'm your daughter, no matter what. I'm sorry you can't change back to a human anymore."

Hearing all that, Lennie started thinking about everything he'd witnessed and became nauseous. The half-can of beer he'd drunk ended up in his throat, so he made for the French doors, to throw up in the shrubs encircling the covered patio. It seemed easier to go there than the half-bath around the corner, between the kitchen and foyer.

Whatever the logic (or lack thereof) of Lennie's choice, no sooner did he open one of the doors and step outside, there was the feeling of soft fur, brushing against his left leg. Lennie glanced down and saw gray-haired Theodore streaking past, making a beeline for the pool area. Once there, the cat scaled the wall and disappeared, undoubtedly soon leaving the property altogether. Then he heard Kit shrieking from inside the house: "No, no, Theodore! You can't leave me!" Afterward she headed for the front door and went outside. Before going in pursuit of her, Lennie finally had to throw up.

Lennie went out the front door, which faced east-west Charter Oak Road, and Kit was nowhere to be seen. Seconds later he heard tires screeching from around the corner, along 96th Street, which ran north and south. His heart felt like it went to his throat, as he considered the possibility Theodore was just hit by a vehicle. What upset Lennie was how devastated Kit would be. In fact she would be more than that, and what he loved most about her was how happy and upbeat she always was. As far as he knew she had little or no family and might have lost some family members in a tragic accident. He never pressed her for any personal information and was determined to be patient. Basically she was obsessed with her cat, and possibly that obsession was hiding an inner pain.

It would have been effortless for Lennie to walk anywhere barefoot in order to come to Kit's aid. However, he didn't have to go farther than the end of the concrete walkway in front of the house before a stranger approached from outside the entry to the property, holding a gray and white cat. That stopped Lennie in his tracks, although he had no idea "who the cat was" for the time being.

As Lennie stared at the beautiful cat, he could hardly keep from crying, yet he couldn't figure out why. Then the stranger said, while still holding the lifeless cat, "A tall, light-blonde-haired woman ran from the front of your house and came right at my car. I'd just veered my car to avoid hitting a cat, which I assume was hers. That cat made it across the street O.K., thanks to me, but like I said, that woman, your wife I guess, ran at my car. But it isn't dented, not even a scratch. The really weird part is your wife somehow ran back in the house while I was getting out of my car. There was obviously a second runaway cat involved, which I must have hit, but I never saw it so I apologize if it was yours or your wife's, too."

By this time Lennie was shaking his head, as he was finally putting two and two (and two) together. Naturally he wasn't about to apprise this stranger of anything. Instead he silently took the cat from the man and thanked him (for what, Lennie still wasn't certain).

Never before had Lennie cried so much as when he carried the cat into the house. He got her fur wet, and it didn't seem like the tears would ever stop.

Kit (as a cat) was cremated. Her remains were in a 14-karat gold urn on the shelf of a side table next to the black leather sofa in Lennie's man cave. At this very moment he was holding the urn against his chest. As much as he wanted to date again, he needed more time (like forever). As much as he wanted a cat, he wasn't sure if he would actually be getting just a cat and not a person, too. Either way, he would be obsessed with cats for the rest of his days.

Sitting Pretty—Not Just for Dogs!

The wind was cold and blustery, hitting James' face as he leaned over the overpass. No, he wasn't about to commit suicide, but he had his dog, Thadeus, with him (long story, that choice of a name). James was actually considering pushing his furry friend off the overpass, onto the busy four-lane highway, below. Was James' life that bad he had to take it out on his dog? That was worse than taking vengeance on himself by committing suicide.

James woke up in a cold sweat, realizing he'd just had a nightmare. Never before was he so happy to be in his bed, even if it was empty. His wife, Michelle, the love of his life, left him for another man, a veterinarian, and she didn't even have a pet! Nonetheless, James was "happy" for her, but he could only fool himself for so long, believing that. He actually feared he might snap at some point. To have a nightmare in which he'd kill his dog, the only one on the planet to give him some hope, confirmed that fear.

What got James the most upset about the "situation" with Michelle, was the fact most of her things were still in the house yet she'd "moved out." Last evening she'd stopped by to pick up some more clothes and admitted she wasn't sure if she was doing the right thing. Since she didn't end up taking much, he held out hope she'd finally realize it was time to come back home.

Michelle's decision to leave James came out of the blue, as far as he was concerned. Maybe he'd simply been in denial about how miserable she was. Her veterinarian lover wasn't

quite as much of a cheater, as he was at least in divorce proceedings with his soon-to-be ex-wife. However, they had
three kids together, so their divorce was probably pretty com-
plicated. James and Michelle didn't have kids because she
never wanted any. He went along with her because he just
wanted to make sure she was happy. He now realized he'd
been wasting his time (trying to make her happy).

James wished he could be angry with her. Maybe he was
secretly relieved. At least there wouldn't be a custody battle
over Thadeus, as she never had time for a pet. Taking care of
herself took up all her spare time. At the same time, it wasn't
like she hated dogs. If she had to take care of Thadeus or
occasionally feed him, it was no big deal for her.

It was hard to believe James had ever considered the possibility he wouldn't mind if his wife cheated on him. The fact
she actually did so was probably what had him so bent out
of shape—the unexpectedness of as much.

Michelle was a great person (despite her indiscretions).
She was smart, beautiful, engaging, enthused about everything...yet she did the one thing he could never forgive. In
turn she made him a cuckold. In the meantime James had
unconditionally loved and respected her. In other words she
basically threw him away.

Dr. Mole? That was her lover's name. No, his first name
sounded like "mole." It was Molan. Molan Grist. He owned
"Valley View Animal Clinic" in Mesa, Arizona. It was kind of
out of James' way to take Thadeus there, but he intended to,
claiming his regular clinic was too busy to take Thadeus that
day.

He'd worry about the question regarding Thadeus' current vaccinations when the time came. The problem was he
didn't want the vet to see his last name, or he might refuse
to see Thadeus (and James). James wanted this visit to be as
much of a surprise as possible.

One thing Michelle did not do was start working at her
lover's vet clinic. Therefore, when James called the clinic at

eight Monday morning, he wasn't worried she might be at the other end of the line. The receptionist identified herself as "Jan," and James told her his dog wasn't feeling well. She didn't ask one question and told him to bring Thadeus in as soon as possible. Since the drive was a good forty minutes, he figured he'd call in at work and claim he was sick. He had a decent work record, so lying a little wouldn't hurt anything, would it?

James had to do a couple things before taking Thadeus to the vet clinic (including calling his workplace), so he wasn't on his way there until almost nine.

Upon arrival, James was amazed to still not be asked for any sort of vaccination record for Thadeus. He had a copy in his pocket but was willing to go along with how this was playing out and "just see what happened." After all, this breach of protocol was playing right into his hands. At the same time, was he, James, falling into a "trap" of Dr. Grist's? He would be finding out soon. The best thing to do was stay calm and play along.

James and Thadeus were ushered into an examination room after waiting for no more than a couple minutes. The vet tech then said, "Dr. Grist will be with you and Thadeus in just a moment."

At first James was incredulous; if this vet clinic was anything like the one he usually took Thadeus to (Sunny Valley Animal Hospital), the wait for Dr. Grist would be longer than just a moment. However, in no time at all Dr. Grist practically burst in the doorway (via the interior of the clinic). He looked right at James and didn't even glance (down) at Thadeus. But he was smiling as he held out his hand, simultaneously introducing himself: "Molan Grist. Very pleased to meet you, Mr. Thornton."

It was impossible for James to immediately reply. Should he say, "Do you know who I am?"; or: "You obviously know who I am!" Maybe this was the best icebreaker: "Hey you cheating, f****** son of a *****!" The latter was definitely along the lines of what James was really thinking.

All the animosity was safely hidden away when James ended up shaking hands with Dr. Grist. James obviously didn't need to bother telling the guy his name. More head games or just doing his job (in regard to Dr. Grist)?

Dr. Grist was very handsome, it must be mentioned. Tall and fit, with wavy, dark-blond hair (and no receding hairline). James wanted to say, "At least Michelle has good taste," but that was like shooting himself in the foot. James had already been humiliated on one front by knowing his wife had left him for the very man standing before him.

For the time being Dr. Grist was all business. After glancing at a piece of paper that had a minimal amount of information about Thadeus (and James), he asked James, "Who is your regular veterinarian?"

"Dr. Cathy Saunders at Sunny Valley Animal Hospital."

Dr. Grist nodded and said, "So she was too busy to see Thadeus on short notice yet he possibly requires immediate attention? What seems to be the problem with him?"

It took about all James had—or so he thought—to break some ice big time and reply, "He's fine-o. The problem is with you."

"Pardon me for asking but how so?"

"You're screwing my wife and she must like it because I don't think she's coming back," James declared, shaking from head to toe by this time. Given Dr. Grist's expression it suddenly seemed possible he hadn't "set up" James at all and was shocked to find himself face-to-face with his lover's husband (and his dog). All this outpouring of emotion had been making James irrational. That thought started to in turn make him feel embarrassed. As it was, what did he really have to lose at this point? Probably the next step (in Dr. Grist's mind) was for Michelle's husband (the guy named James standing in an examination room of his veterinary clinic) to feel neutered, without having to endure the procedure.

MORE DOGS AND THEIR TWISTED TALES– AND ONE CAT STORY

Once all this went through James' head, he suddenly had more confidence, of all things. He proceeded to declare, "I came here to confront you because Michelle's not only moved out but basically shut me out of her life, so I don't even have an opportunity to tell her how much I miss her and would like nothing more than talk to her. I'll tell you right now I feel better already, having told you what I did. And no, I don't approve of you fucking Michelle because she and I are technically still married. Do you even realize that? I mean, you want her so much, could you at least hold off a little until we're divorced? At this rate you'll be sick of her before I can legally get her out of my life. And from what I've heard you're not even divorced yet, either!"

"Get out of my clinic," Dr. Grist told James.

"Gladly," James said and turned to leave, pulling Thadeus' leash to make sure he followed right beside him. Never before was James so happy to make a departure. At least the visit didn't cost him anything, other than most of his dignity.

Molan Grist knew Michelle Thornton (maiden name "Crane") from "way back," as they'd dated in high school. They'd reconnected on a social site and immediately started communicating online. It became "emotional cheating," Molan was the first to agree, but he had already been separated from his wife, Emily. He'd told Michelle the divorce he was going through was messy and was interested in having coffee with a familiar face, just to feel better for a few minutes. Without realizing it he had already been seducing her. They'd met at a cool place right around the corner from his clinic. And the clinic ended up being where they'd meet for "something more" after they'd have coffee. Or they'd skip the coffee and just––.

At first Molan was ashamed and wondered what the hell was he thinking? The more he'd thought about everything, however, his behavior was entirely justified (if he did say so himself). Emily and he had three beautiful daughters and she was a great mom. That was it! Molan never knew he could be so bored out of his mind. Emily was sweet until it was sprung on her, he wanted to live like a bachelor for awhile. The claws came out and she turned into a harridan! Molan never thought that would have happened, considering she didn't have to work, thanks to him.

Once Emily filed the divorce papers, Molan completely let go and had a brazen affair with Michelle, not considering what her husband might think of as much. Obviously that was finally disclosed. The problem was Molan didn't really want Michelle either, not in the long-term (such as marriage). It wasn't like he didn't still have feelings for her. They'd "gone steady" for over two years in high school, practically an eternity at the time. They'd only broken up because he was going away to college, and she still had a year left of high school.

If it looked like James left Valley View Animal Clinic "with his tail between his legs," that wasn't actually the case. He was planning his next move and couldn't afford to waste a minute, deciding what to do. Then again, he'd gotten the day off so he could bring Thadeus with him to meet Michelle's new boyfriend.

Thadeus had to relieve himself before getting back in James' maroon Ford Explorer, so James took him to the grassy area on the east side of the clinic. The next thing he knew, Michelle drove up and parked her white Dodge Durango facing the clinic entryway, ignoring the fact it was a no parking zone. She proceeded to run into the building. James was floored by her tunnel vision. Obviously she was very stressed.

Rather than hurry off, James decided to stick around and see what might transpire in the next couple minutes. He didn't have to wait long before Michelle reappeared and hurriedly got back in her Durango. After starting it, instead of backing up and leaving, she shifted into drive and headed straight for the glass door of the clinic's entrance, which had an off-white brick pillar on either side. James hurried Thadeus to his SUV and attempted to leave before being forced to witness the destruction of the clinic building and/or something else. In all honesty, what did Michelle expect to do with her Durango? It would be totaled long before she did any real damage to her lover's place of business. Besides, the airbags would deploy if she decided to go crazy and ram the building while accelerating.

James didn't depart the parking lot before witnessing Michelle going through with trying to hit the glass entryway door with her vehicle. He heard glass shattering, but it was on Michelle's Durango, nothing else. She managed to get the SUV stuck between the brick pillars and couldn't move it forward anymore nor put it in reverse. The architect of the building was a genius if he'd placed those entryway pillars just so, for an occasion such as this.

Rather than laugh as he drove away from Valley View Animal Clinic, James felt like crying. Then he reminded himself he had his best friend with him, Thadeus. Meanwhile, his estranged wife was literally stuck in the entryway of the clinic.

Since Michelle and Dr. Molan Grist had each other, there was no longer any reason to "plot a next move," as James had formerly determined would take place. As it turned out those two were one another's punishment.

His (and Her) Only Friend

Phil just couldn't seem to help admonishing his wife, Katherine, if good-naturedly. They would be celebrating their 25th wedding anniversary in September, a couple months away. Therefore, it was safe to say he'd been "picking on her" for a long time.

The weather here in Sedona, Arizona, was perfect any time of the year. It never got as hot as it did down in Phoenix, yet the elevation wasn't noticeable, not like it could be in Flagstaff. That meant Phil had one less thing to complain about. Phoenix was his first choice of where to live, yet Katherine couldn't wait to move up here, as soon as he retired from his career in newspaper publishing. She was stuck on the place because of its "supernatural energy." Whatever.

As if to prove how temperate the Sedona weather was here on a late afternoon in mid-July, Phil and Katherine were hosting their guests on the patio of their two-story, log-sided house (versus sitting inside where it was air-conditioned). Joel and Meg Bass were only staying in Sedona for one night, but that wasn't why Katherine didn't want to make up the guest room bed for them. She detested them because they were Phil's friends, and for whatever reason she had zero interest in getting to know them and made no secret of as much, sitting there like a lump. This wasn't the first occasion they'd visited. Usually they flew to Phoenix from Columbus, Ohio and drove up here. Phil's dog, Lodi, was relegated to the indoors because Meg was supposedly allergic to dogs. The problem was she was PETRIFIED of dogs. Phil had no clue why she didn't just say so. It was a good thing he was too irritated with his wife's attitude to call Meg on it, even in jest.

What got Phil the most annoyed on this occasion was why Katherine wasn't completely tight-lipped: she was chain-smoking! With literally nothing to say, she was instead smoking her way through the Basses' visit. On this occasion they had driven all the way from Columbus, making stops along the way to visit family and friends. Their destination was San Diego, where they were spending two weeks at a golf resort before heading back east, taking a more northerly route. (Joel too had since retired.)

If Katherine was jealous of the Basses in any way, it would have been their ability to ride in a vehicle together. Phil couldn't drive a mile with Katherine in the passenger seat before she had to make some sort of remark about his driving skills and driving-related, decision-making ability. As much as he wanted to have fun with her on a road trip, it was impossible. Thankfully Lodi thought he was a great driver and enjoyed himself in the car, every time. Therefore, Phil took Lodi with him for his one or two hour drives in the area (or went alone). That was about his only hobby while Katherine had none!

What Phil would have given to remind Katherine (in front of their current guests) how much he sacrificed when her younger sister, Sheila, showed up every Christmas with her husband, Kyle, and their three kids—Randy, Pamela, and Cindy. Randy was the eldest at fourteen, and Pamela was ten. Their sister was eight. It was a shock having them visit, as Phil and Katherine's son, Phil Junior, was already twenty-five and married, although he didn't leave home until he was twenty-three. Anyway, Phil would make the best of the situation and get along with everyone as well as he could, even taking them on car rides. At least they didn't complain!

Finally Phil could no longer tolerate Katherine's blatant insolence and remarked, "You're always so worried about what the sun does to your skin, yet those damned cigarettes do far more damage, especially when you insist upon smoking one after another."

Phil managed to frost his wife so completely with that one remark the cigarette almost slipped through her fingers—because her hand had frozen up. Meanwhile, since Joel and Meg were both health nuts, they smiled—albeit a bit nervously, following his comment.

Once Katherine recovered from her "shock," she gave Phil dagger looks like he'd never seen before. In that moment he wondered how the hell they'd stayed married for so long.

Katherine finished her cigarette and calmly stood. She then went back in the house, barely bothering to say good-bye to the Basses.

Before leaving, the Basses invited Phil and Katherine to have breakfast at their hotel at eight in the morning. Phil told them he'd see them then, leaving it "open" whether Katherine would get her act together enough to ride in the car with him for two miles and then sit through breakfast with a couple she obviously didn't like. Was that too much to ask? It remained to be seen.

Naturally Phil had needlessly gotten his hopes up about Katherine joining him and the Basses for a buffet breakfast at "Red Rock Resort and Spa." She not only wouldn't go, she decided not to bother getting out of bed—at least not in a timely manner, which she usually did. Of course she had an excuse, claiming she had a migraine. She used that for everything! Come to think of it she did this last year when they'd visited. On that occasion, however, Phil and Katherine had been invited to the hotel for lunch and dinner, but she was only "available" for dinner. She had absolutely nothing to do all day! To top it off she ended up going someplace for a couple hours and looked disheveled when she did finally return.

On this occasion, Phil was so disgusted with Katherine he didn't even say good-bye before leaving the house. It was unlikely she was asleep, so she would be furious with him. Because of that he called everything even and was on his way. However, he did tell Lodi good-bye and said he'd be back to pick him up for a drive after breakfast. It was doubtful Katherine heard the exchange because the bedroom door was closed, and Phil was with Lodi downstairs, having just taken him outside for a short walk. As it was, Phil didn't feel as if any sort of apology was in order. Thanks to his immense success as a newspaper publisher for many years, he was able to walk away from the dying business, his fortune (in relative terms) intact. Nowadays he wrote freelance articles here and there, mostly to satisfy his urge to spout off about something, good-naturedly, just like he did with his wife, regarding "picking on her." Doing so could never have any effect on her. After all, he was doing it under the pretense of "kidding," and Katherine certainly knew by now he meant no harm.

Breakfast with the Basses was very enjoyable. Phil was the only one concerned about the absence of his wife. They didn't appear to be the least bit surprised Katherine was a no-show, yet they were completely disinterested in talking about what a b—ch she was being. Phil wanted to vent about her so much he could hardly stand it, simultaneously aware it was uncalled for. Obviously they were looking forward to reaching their vacation destination in San Diego, to relax and play golf. Besides, they were accustomed to her rudeness by this time.

Driving home, Phil suddenly became so drowsy he almost fell asleep. Unfortunately he happened to have been nearing an intersection where the light had just changed. How he didn't rear end the vehicle in front of his was nothing short of a miracle. At least the episode woke him up.

Having previously wanted to take a post-breakfast drive, Phil was thinking perhaps he ought to go home and take a nap. It wasn't as if he was tired; he got plenty of sleep the night before. Initially he'd intended to stop at home and pick up Lodi for the drive. Maybe it was better to just get the drive out of the way and then go home. Lodi wouldn't know the difference. As for Katherine, the longer Phil stayed away from the house, the better. By the time he did return, hopefully her headache would be gone, along with her anger with him for having failed to tell her good-bye.

Phil took an hour drive that consisted of a particularly enjoyable route, and he pulled into the driveway of his house feeling greatly refreshed. Maybe part of the problem lately was he took Katherine's sour moods too personally. To be honest, time (along with her smoking habit) had not been kind to her looks. It was a good thing she wasn't an outdoors-type, or she'd look even more haggard than she did. That sounded shallow, but it wasn't like he'd ever cheat on her. Instead he shut himself off—and spent more time than ever taking drives—usually with Lodi.

Oops. Phil hadn't meant to describe his wife so negatively. However, at forty-nine, she looked at least ten years older, and she had to know he didn't approve of her appearance. He was fifty himself and liked to think he looked good for his age. Katherine's appearance indicated what she really thought of herself—as far as Phil was concerned. Maybe it was genetically impossible for her to age well.

Phil came back to reality the second he unlocked the front door, and Lodi started barking. Lodi knew who was entering the house, even before seeing his owner. Once inside, Phil ended up following Lodi upstairs, expecting the worst about his wife.

The second Phil opened the bedroom door, Lodi ran straight to the closed sliding door of the walk-in closet. Nonetheless, Lodi started barking again at it, crazy dog! Phil's concern was centered on Katherine, who was still in bed, the covers over her head. Her body didn't appear to have moved since when he'd left earlier. As worried as he was about her welfare, he was also slightly irritated, having been reminded of how unmotivated she always was.

Death creeped Phil out as it was, and he suddenly found it impossible to pull the covers away from Katherine's face. What if there was a horrific expression on her face? He'd never be the same if he was forced to witness that. Should he call an ambulance? If she really was still sleeping, she'd be more furious than ever with him.

Meanwhile, Lodi was still barking at the closed closet door. Phil told him, "Enough already, Lodi!" That got him to shut up, but he remained by the door and paced in tiny circles in front of it.

Finally Phil couldn't take it anymore, and he stood beside the bed, pulling the covers back. He nearly screamed upon seeing Katherine's head had turned into a dog's, resembling a Rottweiler. The transformation must have killed her, as she was completely immobile and didn't appear to be breathing. He dared to touch her face, and the fur was real! He started pulling on it, expecting to remove a mask or heavily applied makeup, but nothing happened. Meanwhile she neither moved nor twitched. This was apparently not a joke. He always had a suspicion the supernatural powers in the area could cause something totally inexplicable to take place. That and the fact Katherine loved to dabble in the occult and enjoyed going to tarot card readings. Evidently she'd gone to one too many.

"Come on, Lodi, let's get out of here," Phil told his dog. Fortunately Lodi knew to obey his master at a time like this because Phil's patience level was at zero. "We're going on a car ride to Phoenix. We're better off down there, permanently. It's all Katherine's fault we ended up moving here, since she had such an aversion to the heat in the summer. Felt fine to me, any day or season. Lodi, you're my best friend if only because you end up agreeing with me, like it or not. I'll have all our possessions sent to us. It's not like I can't afford to indulge, especially at a time like this."

It wasn't like Phil couldn't afford it was right. That was Katherine's take on the matter, which was how she got the house here in Sedona as part of their divorce settlement. Joel Bass was moving in with her as soon as his divorce was "finalized," and he could leave Ohio (and his ex-wife, Meg) for good. It seemed like it was taking forever. They kept in touch via lots of texts and e-mails, which was how they'd kept in contact between "visits" over the years. Katherine got turned on just thinking about how their respective spouses never suspected a thing. That had made their trysts all the more illicit (and enjoyable). She couldn't wait until Joel finally arrived because she was so lonely. It never occurred to her how empty the house would be without even Lodi around. She hesitated to get a dog because she didn't want the bother of taking care of it. That sounded so lazy, but she was, which irritated Phil. She didn't miss him, but she felt like she should. Their son wasn't even speaking to her at this point because his parents' divorce was "her fault." She had no way to clear her name because the only obvious factor in the split was she'd been having an affair. All Phil's emotional abuse was magically swept under the rug. However, Katherine was well-aware there was no excuse for her behavior.

The more she thought about everything, Katherine was better off getting a dog and permanently dumping the lover who couldn't seem to finalize his divorce. It had been easy enough for her and Phil to divorce, so what was the problem with Joel? Was he even being truthful?

As it was, Phil was the one who'd initiated the divorce proceedings. It was a little-known fact because Katherine was too respectful of him to try and explain "the truth" to their son. The "joke" involving the dog mask and how realistic it was, was what got Phil, not the fact she'd been having an ongoing affair with his friend. If anything, Phil was somewhat understanding and even relieved to find out Katherine had acted insolent in the Basses' presence so her cover wouldn't be blown. (Perhaps Phil was even titillated by what he'd found out?) Anyway, her affair could have been forgiven, if only she'd hadn't exposed him for being extremely gullible.

It was all Lodi's fault everything came crashing down the way it did. Also, Phil hadn't ended up taking quite as long of a drive as Katherine had expected. It hadn't helped, Joel suddenly didn't want to leave, the more he considered having to spend two weeks in San Diego playing golf—and being alone with Meg. He feared finally coming clean with her and was actually considering confronting Phil about the whole thing, first. At the last second he changed his mind, and that was when Katherine whipped out her dog mask. She'd ordered it online a couple years ago, specifically for an occasion such as this. What she'd intended to do was wear it to distract her husband for a minute so Joel could make his escape. What she hadn't counted on was Lodi barging in on them ahead of Phil. Joel's plan to hide in the closet almost didn't work. Anyway, Phil ended up leaving because he initially believed her head had been turned into a dog's! He admitted as much when Katherine later came clean with him about everything. She felt like she deserved some credit if only for having lay on her back in an authentic-looking dog mask, trying to look dead. It was difficult to breathe in that thing.

Revisiting the notion of getting a dog....It made more sense to do that than keep waiting around for her lover. Katherine might even have to swear off men altogether. While she was at it, she'd try to like driving (versus being afraid). Phil never realized she had a fear of driving and was completely impatient with her. She was never in a car accident, which would have been the most logical explanation for this fear.

Katherine could take her new dog (or puppy) for car rides. Finally she'd have a real friend, accepting her unconditionally and not criticizing her for everything.

Her Sister's Lover—Or Her Killer?

Even if some identical twins think alike, that wasn't the case for the Fehrer sisters, Julianne and Sarah. One of the most striking differences between the two twenty-eight-year-olds was Sarah was indifferent to everyone except herself—and her string of boyfriends, of course. Even though Sarah claimed to want to settle down and start a family, her behavior indicated otherwise. The problem was there were individuals who didn't approve of her lifestyle and were perhaps jealous. Julianne liked to think she knew not to make a man jealous, so she only had monogamous relationships. At the same time she made no pretenses about "settling down" because she recently broke up with yet another boyfriend. Two years appeared to be as long as she could stay with a guy before one or the other decided to break things off. There was never a huge argument, although she was furious with her latest boyfriend, Jack Donaught, for telling her it was over because she'd "started acting more weird and OCD ever since Sarah was murdered." Hello! What did he expect? Sarah was killed in her Scottsdale, Arizona apartment six months ago, and the killer was still on the loose. Authorities had concluded she must have known her killer, as there wasn't a forced entry. Nothing was removed from the premises, so the individual had visited her apartment to take her life and nothing else. Maybe Julianne was still in shock, as she still couldn't wrap her head around exactly what had happened.

It was a shame Sarah didn't have time for anything but

herself and her boyfriends. If she had a dog, like Julianne did, maybe he could have protected her that fateful afternoon? Then again, since Sarah supposedly knew her killer...

If Jack thought Julianne was so weird, did he ever consider she also lost her mother to cancer barely a year ago? However, that wasn't a total shock, as she had been ill for a couple years. Not to say it was a relief she passed away, but she had been miserable for a long time. If she had still been alive when Sarah was murdered, that would have sent her over the edge.

The investigation of Sarah's murder was "ongoing," which Julianne took to mean the cops hadn't entirely given up but needed some help at this point. Julianne would have been happy to help, as she just quit her latest job, working at a stationery store. (Yes, they still exist.) As it was, she had been questioned on a couple occasions by Detective Redmond. Following each interrogation he'd given her a business card with his name and contact information. The first time he'd handed her a card, she almost made a joke, such as, "I never knew cops carried business cards. Imagine that!" Maybe she would have been flirting without even realizing it, as he was awfully cute. Even though he had to be a few years older than herself and was wearing a wedding band, there was a boyish demeanor about him that compelled her "to let her guard down."

If Sarah had the opportunity to voice her opinion, she would have told Julianne to "go for it." In other words, an affair with a married man was fun! Not only that, you didn't have to worry about having to put up with his daily habits because they were his wife's problems, first.

Julianne wished she could have agreed with her sister. Sarah and she had different "moral obligations," if you will. Detective Redmond had told Julianne, "If you ever need to talk, call me anytime." Initially she'd thought he was concerned about her, since she'd lost her sister to a murderer and not too long ago lost her mother to cancer. Then she thought maybe he was in fact making an innuendo. After much debate, however, she concluded he wasn't interested in her at all and wanted her to confess to murdering her own sister. Unbelievable! To think this guy probably took special classes and who knew what shit to learn how to nab a killer and that was the best he could do? Given the number of boyfriends Sarah had at any one point, it was a safe bet one of them was jealous and took her life. Case closed, once Detective Redmond picked the right guy. Julianne thought Gil Johnstone was the guilty party, as he was the most accomplished in Sarah's stable of studs, yet he was most likely controlling. Even though both of them had agreed not to be exclusive, they only ended up making each other jealous, particularly Gil.

Having a dog provided an excuse to go outside and take a walk (and have protection). Besides, no one was as noticeable "walking a dog," versus just walking. Julianne's condominium happened to be a mere two blocks from the popular "Fifth Avenue Shops," which were enjoyable to walk past any time of year. However, they were the most interesting during "tourist season" (the cooler months of the year). The art galleries were open late on Thursday evenings, and Julianne loved to take her Corgi mix Cecil for walks then. Little did she know it would turn out to be an eye-opening experience, particularly when passing "Gallery Unique," on the other side of the street. It appeared to have both bronze sculptures and watercolor paintings as its artistic offerings, but the proprietor was the "piece" that really got Julianne going. There was one problem (which Julianne discovered during a late afternoon walk with Cecil the next day): her sister had already "discovered" him. Julianne might have known. Julianne had texted her sister that evening, asking if she'd been with the guy who ran Gallery Unique. Sarah identified Gil Johnstone as the gallery owner. She then asked if Julianne had been walking Cecil at the time. Julianne had wanted to text her back: "Yeah. And I wanted to strangle you with his leash!"

MORE DOGS AND THEIR TWISTED TALES–
AND ONE CAT STORY

Since that was the truth, Julianne simply texted the first part.

Not long after seeing her sister making out with the art gallery owner Julianne had already picked out as "just her type" (having thus far only gotten a look at him from a distance), she started losing interest in her job—to the point she kept calling in sick. In the meantime she took Cecil on more walks past Gallery Unique, including right past it, hoping to run into Gil. Julianne knew little about him, and Sarah never disclosed much about her boyfriends, other than never tiring of pointing out she couldn't be monogamous with any of them. As it was the two sisters were hardly close, and their physical identicalness was about all they had in common. However, they both had a "competitive" relationship—which included how they dressed, who they dated, etc. It nauseated Julianne to try and keep up with Sarah, but it was plain Sarah was "all in," and Julianne did not like losing in any way whatsoever, regarding anything! (Julianne had long ago resigned herself to the fact she was different from most people—including her sister.)

Soon Julianne lost her job—and she didn't care. Besides, she had sufficient finances "to stalk her intended" and would worry about getting another job, later. The inheritance from their mother had allowed her a somewhat take it or leave it attitude about employment, although it was important for her to have the responsibility of going to work someplace.

Sarah had bragged about how she had Gil wanting them to be exclusive, but she wanted her freedom. That bothered Julianne because she would have been thrilled to be Gil Johnstone's "one and only." Julianne wasn't sure how Sarah had met the guy, while Julianne was "reduced" to walking past his gallery. Undoubtedly he'd been questioned by the police after Sarah's murder, but he obviously had yet to be arrested. Maybe he was so smooth he could get away with anything, including murder. Julianne wanted to talk to him, even if it wasn't much more than "hello." It was a start. The guy must have traveled abroad, as he was nowhere to be seen, month after month. Perhaps he was lying low because he was guilty of murder? Before Sarah's death it seemed like he was always popping outside the gallery, whether it was to water the flowers in the terra cotta pots on either side of the doorway or take a call on his cell phone. Admittedly, ever since Sarah's murder Julianne had made a point of only walking past Gallery Unique if she and Cecil remained across the street. She vowed if Gil did appear she'd cross the street with Cecil and introduce herself. The mere thought made her nervous, so maybe she was secretly "relieved" there had been no sight of him? No! She was nervous because she'd picked him out but her sister had already been seeing him. However, Sarah was gone, so it was Julianne's turn! Julianne hadn't even accepted another date ever since breaking up with her ex, Jack, because her mind was completely taken up with Gil.

The truth of the matter was Julianne was literally consumed with meeting Gil Johnstone face-to-face and felt like she was back in junior high, enduring a crush on a guy in seventh grade (she was in sixth). It took him until eighth grade to even notice her and amazingly he did, instead of noticing her sister first, what usually happened. Sarah was always first, one way or another. She even managed to die first. That really irritated Julianne, now that she thought about it.

The time to strike (meet Gil Johnstone) had to take place soon, or Julianne would literally lose her mind. Hopefully he would be returning soon from wherever he went. The Thursday night art walk would be starting up again this very evening, October 1st. Julianne couldn't wait until then to walk Cecil past Gallery Unique and was going to drive down there this morning and go right in the gallery, like she was a customer. (Was that the right word to describe herself or was "stalker" more appropriate?) She had nothing to do, having never even bothered to find another job. She'd spent her free time in the past six months, scouring the Internet for information about Gil Johnstone. It turned out he essentially flew under the radar. Did his possible involvement with Sarah's murder have anything to do with his lack of online presence?

As it was, Julianne was curious to see Gil's reaction when he laid eyes on her. If he had indeed murdered Sarah, he'd probably exclaim, "Didn't I kill you once already?" He'd be too indignant to be fearful. It was unlikely he was aware Sarah had an identical twin because the last thing Sarah would ever do was talk about someone besides herself.

Just as Julianne was checking her watch to make sure it was ten (when Gallery Unique opened), the glass entryway door was opened by none other than "him."

"Hello there," Gil Johnstone said to his first customer of the day, motioning for her to come inside his art gallery and have a look around, which she couldn't wait to do. He couldn't resist staring at her behind as she sauntered past him. She was none other than his girlfriend Sarah's twin sister, who he didn't even know existed until after Sarah's murder. Sarah was a hopeless flirt, that was most likely her demise. As much as he'd wanted them to be exclusive (Gil was prepared to become monogamous thanks to her), she just laughed. It wasn't something he took personally, although there were guys who would.

Detective Josh Redmond was in fact the one who disclosed to Gil, Sarah had an identical twin sister. Gil had been questioned by him the day after Sarah's murder. Another guy in a suit came with the detective and looked around the gallery, looking really angry the whole time. Gil was ready to shit he was so afraid he was about to be framed or something. What would stop them from just hauling him away? As it was he'd in fact spent part of the night before with Sarah, at her apartment. He'd had to leave because his cat Dooley was at home, waiting for him. Oh and another girlfriend,

Mirna, who wanted to move in with him, but he wouldn't even give her a key. (He'd let her in and then told her he had to leave again.) She was past tired of his excuses as to where he was always running off to, as there were only so many art walks he could be hosting at his gallery.

It didn't say much for Gil's character, but he had a solid alibi for where he was about the time Sarah was murdered—at home in bed with his "other girlfriend." Mirna was questioned too, but Gil had no idea where that had occurred or what she was asked. All he knew was she must have said the right things because he had yet to be arrested—not that he was guilty. Since losing Sarah, he was trying to learn to love Mirna, instead.

After Gil had been questioned by Detective Redmond and given what he considered the "all clear" (he wasn't arrested) he was given the following order: If Julianne Fehrer ever came in the gallery, Gil was supposed to act like he didn't recognize her. That didn't sound too difficult, considering the fact he'd never actually met Julianne nor had Sarah made any mention of her. However, he was aware seeing her face-to-face might make the situation more trying.

Gil caught up to where Julianne was, admiring a large watercolor painting of horses grazing in a field. It hung in the middle of the gallery, on a seven-foot wide, white brick support pillar. The other side of it had a painting as well. The entire gallery was about fifteen hundred square feet and had a pine wood floor.

Julianne rarely took the time to gaze at works of art, so it was mentally exerting for her to pretend to be interested doing so for even a few minutes. Then Gil approached her from behind and started revealing some of the background of the artist who painted the watercolor titled "Grazing Horses." She could have sworn he was about to put his arms around her when the phone rang in the back of the gallery.

"Be right back," Gil said and left.

Not ten seconds after Gil disappeared in the back of the

gallery, the front door opened and in strutted a tall, thin brunette, hair pulled back in a high, tight ponytail. If her hair were hanging loose it would have fallen halfway down her back. It was plain she had an attitude, and Julianne was super-glad both were customers and didn't have to deal with each other. To ensure Julianne didn't have to look at the woman, she moved to the other side of the brick support pillar. Hopefully the woman just needed a word with Gil and would leave afterward. As it was, Julianne had hoped to spend a few minutes chatting with Gil, fully expecting to immediately win him over, whether or not he might be into the fact she was Sarah's twin. Possibly that would creep him out a little at first, but he'd get over it. He'd better.

Gil emerged from the back of the gallery and exclaimed, "Mirna, my lovely, what brings you here?"

Julianne rolled her eyes at the description of that bitch. Obviously Mirna did something right in bed last night. The real question was whether Gil had forgotten Julianne was still in the gallery? She decided the best thing to do was remain right where she was—out of plain sight.

"Lock the door for a few," Mirna said, as the two embraced and kissed. (Julianne could tell by the sounds, that was what they were doing; she didn't need to sneak a peek.) "I finally figured out coming here, no pun intended, was my best shot for getting some actual alone time with you."

"Oh, no," Gil said as he detected movement behind the oversized brick pillar that doubled as a room divider, simultaneously "recalling" none other than Julianne Fehrer, a very jealous murderess, was in here with them. The shit part was the phone call that just tied him up for a couple minutes was from Detective Redmond, wanting to know if Gil had any updates on the whereabouts of Julianne Fehrer, as in had she stopped by the gallery? Gil had made the mistake of telling him Julianne was in fact there at the moment, so

Detective Redmond launched into several possible "what if" scenarios, while Gil should have been back out on the gallery floor.

Mirna was never subtle, so if Gil tried to subtlety get her to do something, it probably wouldn't work. Nonetheless he was desperate, so he whispered this in her ear: "I need you to leave right now. It has to do with something potentially very serious. Please?"

Rather than calmly obey Gil, Mirna jumped away from him, exclaiming, "Fuck you! I'm not going anywhere unless I leave with you! Do you think I'm stupid?"

The second Gil heard Mirna make a reference to her possible stupidity, typically a temper tantrum wasn't far behind. Her number one sticking point was having her intelligence level questioned. Was it ever necessary to state the obvious about someone?

Mirna decided to launch into a tirade about how Gil had been leading her on all this time and was never interested in having a serious relationship with her. The proof was the fact he hardly had any time for her.

Gil caught himself nodding, of all things, at a time like this!

"Oh you #@&*!" Mirna yelled and then went on and on after that with more obscenities.

Julianne finally couldn't endure hearing any more of the slander hurled at Gil and came out of hiding to exclaim, "I've heard enough! Who are you to talk, given how pathetic you obviously are!" Then she proceeded to yank on Mirna's ponytail, which caused her to cry as if she were being decapitated. Julianne would have loved to have done the honors. It must have been Mirna's own hair, given how hard Julianne pulled yet nothing came out. Julianne had assumed the bitch was wearing extensions and had wanted to demoralize her by eliminating more than a foot of hair length with just one tug. Oh well.

MORE DOGS AND THEIR TWISTED TALES–
AND ONE CAT STORY

For Thursday night's art walk, Gallery Unique had a sign on its front door: "Due to Circumstances Beyond Gallery Unique's control, it will be closed for the Thursday Evening Art Walk. See you Friday at Ten!"

Meanwhile, Gil had called Detective Redmond back and told him Julianne Fehrer had left again, shortly after her arrival. Gil was implored to call Detective Redmond "if anything new" came up. Gil assured him he would.

And Gil had plenty "new" to report, except he was currently in bed with none other than Julianne Fehrer, the number one suspect in her sister's murder. (Their tryst was the reason for the cancellation of the Thursday night art walk, the first of the latest tourist season.) Suffice to mention, after witnessing Julianne's "heroics" when it came to physically defending Gil against his ex-girlfriend Mirna's verbal attack, how the hell couldn't he be so turned on he couldn't keep his hands off her? Besides, she was the identical twin to the woman he'd wanted to marry!

Gil was ready to forgive Julianne for killing her sister, although he wasn't certain she did it; an irate, vindictive ex of Sarah's probably did. The only thing that made Gil slightly uncertain was the fact her own dog seemed like he was trying to tell Gil something, with his eyes. Tomorrow night, Gil would invite Julianne over and tell her to bring Cecil. The dog could meet Gil's cat, Dooley, and hopefully the two would get along (and compare notes). Dooley could let Gil know what to do with Julianne.

She Would Have Been Better Off Alone

Carlie Jones wanted to be devastated her boyfriend, Larry Gremble, said he didn't want to see her anymore when she told him she was pregnant. Of course it was his kid, that wasn't the issue. She was jubilant of all things, because his attitude gave her a good idea what kind of man he was. She was thirty-five to his forty-five, and neither one had ever married (or so he claimed).

Fortunately Carlie had sufficient financial stability, so she didn't have to expect Larry to "help out" (but it would have been welcomed nonetheless). Again, his actions appeared to show what his character was. They had dated for almost a year when "this" happened, and Carlie took the blame. She'd gotten reckless and had determined she was at the age when it started to become difficult to get pregnant. It was obviously an unwanted pregnancy for Larry, but she was determined to be optimistic. It helped Carlie's mother, Bonnie, was very supportive and lived only a couple miles from Carlie's house in Scottsdale, Arizona. Bonnie worked for a non-profit agency, and she did much of her work from home. She could watch the baby at her place while Carlie was at work, or she could babysit at Carlie's.

Maybe the time Carlie picked to tell Larry she was pregnant, was what had turned him off: right after they'd had sex! The problem was she was barely showing but had turned into a nymphomaniac. She'd begged him to come over last night, and he actually stayed until morning. He was shocked she "wanted it again" and afterward, she broke the news.

There was no taking anything back at this point, and Carlie could only move on. She was more accepting she was going to be a mom than her ex (?) boyfriend's reaction to as much.

Carlie's mother wasn't bothered by the fact her daughter planned on raising the baby on her own, as she, Bonnie, had divorced Carlie and her brother Corey's father when the former was ten, the latter, five. No longer was Melvin even alive, having passed away close to a decade ago. Suffice to mention, news of his death didn't elicit much of a reaction from either Carlie or Corey. Carlie liked her job and planned on working as long as possible, up until her due date. She also intended to return to work ASAP, not letting having a baby crimp her work schedule any more than was absolutely necessary. If this sounded callous as far as her "anticipation" of motherhood, she had a lot of conflicting emotions with which to grapple. Larry's initial reaction to being a father helped make Carlie ambivalent about her predicament. She wished she could quit being attracted to good-looking but shallow men.

Larry was in shock, was all. Once the news really sunk in, he'd be thrilled. He might even send Carlie a bouquet, with a note congratulating her. Despite her determination to "go it alone," she wanted to know she had his moral support, at the very least.

Carlie's best friend, Melissa Rogers, was the only other person who knew about Carlie's pregnancy besides Larry, Bonnie and Corey. Melissa had a ten-year-old daughter, Amanda, with her husband, Todd. Carlie always thought Todd was an a-hole but kept the opinion to herself because Melissa worshipped him. As it was, Carlie had a horrible track record with men.

The Rogers family was moving to California in a few months, and Todd had determined the puppy Melissa had recently purchased for their daughter, would have to go (but not with them). That sounded cruel, all the way around. Carlie's pregnancy news had been a bright spot for Melissa, and she'd effusively congratulated Carlie. Carlie remembered there being a dog in the Jones' house until about the time her parents split up. Carlie couldn't say for sure, but it was possible her father took the little black mutt with him when he left. There was never another dog in the household, and Carlie didn't blame her mother at all, raising two kids on her own and having a full-time job.

Why was Carlie so worried about a dog that wasn't even hers? It had to be her hormones doing this, nothing more.

Carlie worked at Emerald Desert Inn, in Paradise Valley. Since she had an office job, there was no concern about her appearance, such as if she were a hostess. That was what Melissa did, at the hotel's "Le Noble" restaurant. Carlie's boss, Ron Port, had no idea she was pregnant, yet he looked at her differently today when she arrived. She couldn't wait to get behind her desk and even neglected to pop in Le Noble and say hello to Melissa, like she usually did. Soon Carlie would have no choice but to disclose the news to Ron. She'd worked here for close to six years, longer than Ron had been here. Sue Matthews had been her prior boss, and she was harder to work for than he was. Ron was much more easygoing. The owner, Jay Somerfield, Carlie had yet to meet. Rumor had it he was a plastic surgery fanatic, but that wasn't the whole story. Shamelessly curious, she wished she knew more about him.

Usually Ron took a lunch break and disappeared for a good hour. That would be Carlie's opportunity to get up and stretch and use the restroom. She'd brought a sack lunch with a few items (all nutritious), so she could remain right at her desk. Besides, she wanted to e-mail Larry when she had a few minutes, ask him how he was feeling. She expected some sort of reply from the father of her baby, or she would be incensed.

At ten-thirty Carlie received an e-mail from none other

than Daddy-O, and he had this to say: "I just wanted to let you know, ever since you told me you're going to make us parents, I haven't been able to think about ANYTHING ELSE! And I don't mean that in a good way, so don't get all excited. I have to think about it all some more, and I will try to make some sense of it. You should be really happy I'm even bothering to do this because I never wanted kids, not even one!"

Carlie was accustomed to having Larry talk to her like this, so just the fact she received an e-mail from him was practically a gift, never mind how rude he was. So determined was she to "make this whole thing work," it was impossible for her to notice he was such a selfish jerk, she was better off cutting her losses, right then and there! Instead, she got excited when she proceeded to receive a second e-mail from him. To think, she didn't have to initiate communication with him!

Larry tried to lay it on thick (but not too thick) this morning in a second e-mail to his girlfriend, Carlie, he wasn't going to "just accept" the fact she got knocked-up, all because she was too stupid to take some sort of precaution. As it was, Larry liked to think he only had relationships with "responsible" females. That was a real sticking point for Larry, not the realization a baby was on the way. Little did Carlie know, she'd have two babies to take care of when Larry moved in with her. The news at work was guys like Larry, a pharmaceutical representative who was considered "old," would have their jobs eliminated by the end of the year. He'd been eyeing retirement since he turned forty, five years ago, so this wasn't exactly the worst news. He was about to become Mr. Mom, although Carlie had no idea how much of a leech he intended to be. (It was better that way.) He was aware she wanted him "to be in the picture," despite her weak attempts at appearing independent.

In case Larry sounded as if he was secretly a lazy slob, he needed to clarify something: he would look for employment while caring for their tyke but would do so at his leisure. He figured the baby would spend most of his or her time sleeping anyway. He was aware Carlie's mother was planning on clearing her schedule in order to do plenty of grandchild bonding, but she could ease off on her eagerness. Larry came before her in decisions for the newborn's life, so if he wanted to do ALL the babysitting, he would, damn it! In the meantime he would be moving out of his luxury condo and into his bachelor-brother Eaton's penthouse in a downtown Phoenix skyscraper, waiting for his time to make a "permanent" appearance. Eaton happened to be between girlfriends, so he would be letting Larry crash on his sofa sleeper for a few months. The last thing Larry could "afford" to do was let Carlie know how financially precarious his situation was. Evidently she was better at keeping a budget than he was. Her salary couldn't have been that great, working at Emerald Desert Inn, but she had an above-average house in Scottsdale, not far from her mother's, which was where Carlie and her brother Corey grew up. Corey was a rock star wannabe who played at some decent local venues. Since she helped arrange gigs for him, maybe she got a percentage of his income. There was simply no other way to explain how she seemed to live so well. Having Larry mooch off her was exactly what she deserved for thoughtlessly getting pregnant. It wasn't fair to the kid to say Carlie deserved outright punishment, but she kind of did.

Meanwhile, Larry's financial downfall had been thanks to his total lack of discipline when it came to spending money, so he was getting his own punishment. He had no one to blame but himself, but since he was going to be losing his well-paying job pretty soon, why not blame everyone else instead? It almost made losing, fun.

That evening, Carlie had no appetite but was making something for dinner anyway. Besides, cooking always calmed her, and right now she was stressed. By the way, wasn't she supposed to be hungry all the time? When would that aspect of being pregnant kick in?

Larry had ended up sending Carlie plenty of e-mails at work, not one of them indicating he was welcoming the aspect of becoming a father. Instead, he couldn't seem to get enough of complaining about how much she'd inconvenienced him by getting pregnant. He sounded as if he was trying to set himself up for something. She was always up for surprises, if that wasn't already pretty evident.

Carlie was about to sit down to eat, and Larry called. Instead of answering the phone, she decided whatever he wanted to tell her could wait until after dinner. Before long they would be sitting across from one another at this very table in the kitchen of her house, provided he was "serious" about moving in with her after she had the baby. A lot could happen in the meantime, particularly regarding his employment. With the constantly changing healthcare laws, it was possible his position would become obsolete—or so Larry claimed.

As Carlie was finishing eating, Larry called again. A favorite TV show of hers was about to begin, so she'd call him back after it was over. No, he'd start calling her in lesser and lesser time increments if she didn't either answer now or call him right back. In the evening he called her, versus texting or e-mailing, because he knew she was sitting around doing nothing anyway and liked to talk. That was admittedly true. However, she did not want to chat with him if he was going to be combative with her, which she feared he would.

Then Carlie's mother called. Carlie answered the phone this time. Afterward, Bonnie asked her how she was feeling, to which Carlie replied, "Fine."

"That's it?"

Carlie was trying to keep it simple, O.K.? Surely her mother didn't want to hear Carlie's list of gripes, so Carlie said, "Yes, Mom, that's it."

"O.K. then," Bonnie said. "How's things going with

Larry?"

Carlie was afraid to answer with "Fine" because her mother would never settle for that. How about: CARLIE DID NOT WANT TO DISCUSS ANYTHING ABOUT LARRY. And she definitely didn't want to do so with her mother, who did not like Larry and was all for him being "a thing of the past."

Carlie's phone beeped, as there was an incoming call. She welcomed the excuse to get off the phone but did tell her mother why. Fortunately her mother was used to this kind of thing and didn't take it personally.

Bonnie was "proud" to say neither one of her kids seemed to have time for her anymore, as she liked to think that was proof of their success. Therefore she was jumping at the opportunity to babysit, once Carlie had her baby! It didn't bother Bonnie the child would be born out of wedlock; the pregnancy must have been what Carlie wanted, despite not being married to the father. As it was, Carlie had constantly complained about him but was obviously attracted to him nonetheless. Bonnie could easily identify with how her daughter felt. And Bonnie's two pregnancies were certainly "intentional," although she was married. Anymore, however, marriage hardly seemed relevant, whether or not kids were involved. Bonnie had known her marriage wouldn't last because her husband had too short of an attention span for maintaining a relationship.

Melissa had no idea the favor she did Carlie by calling her, having considered texting her but was dealing with a very emotional issue. Texting didn't seem like the most appropriate way to communicate, although she was so upset it was hard to keep from crying, which could make it impossible to talk.

Anyway, Carlie didn't immediately pick up, so Melissa was preparing to leave a voicemail. When Carlie did answer, she was happy to hear from Melissa, which helped the situation. However, Melissa immediately killed any positive emotions by tearfully declaring, "Todd has decided Oscar has to leave tonight! He nipped at Todd after Todd tried to grab him and throw him outside because he peed on the floor. And Oscar only peed on the floor because Todd yelled at him when he got home from work. We were going to put him up for adoption but Todd wants to dump him at Chaparral Park. Amanda ran into her bedroom, crying, and won't come out."

"I'll take Oscar," Carlie said.

Melissa was thrilled.

Finally Carlie could no longer hide her pregnancy from her boss, Ron. He'd finally ambushed her the other morning, when it had become impossible for her to sneak into the office, although she no longer took a detour first to see Melissa because she had already moved to California with her family. He took one look at Carlie and asked, "Is that why you've been hiding from me?" After she sheepishly nodded, he congratulated her and proceeded to ask when she intended to take a leave of absence. Initially she was caught off-guard by the question, but he was only doing his job. Carlie told him she wanted to work "as long as possible." Ron said that was fine, but he needed a few weeks' notice she would need time off well before she went into labor, making it clear it looked to him like she was ready to burst.

Carlie hated to do it, but she gave Ron notice right at that moment. She felt badly about having waited, as it was obvious he was angry with her but pretended he wasn't. However, she made it clear she intended to return to work as soon as two weeks after having the baby.

Ron's reply to that was, "We'll see."

Carlie told him, "No 'we' won't. I'll be back then. I'll have help taking care of the baby, so I won't have a problem."

"Are you sure about that?"

"Yes."

"If you say so."

As it turned out, Carlie was able to keep her word, and Larry came through for her as well. He moved in shortly after she came home from the hospital with their son, Joey. For a second it appeared her house might be a little crowded, as her mother went out of her way to be helpful, while Larry was suddenly determined to be attentive to her every need. It wasn't as great as it sounded because Carlie knew Larry could never go the distance, being so solicitous. Meanwhile, her mother might get pissed off he was hanging around so much and wouldn't be available when Carlie needed her to babysit. After all, Carlie expected Larry to get a job, although he did mention doing something "home-based." That was great, but did he have a plan? Early on, he'd mentioned being a full time babysitter for Joey, but not for a minute did she expect him to be serious. And all this conjecturing came about because he did indeed lose his pharmaceutical job, which was eliminated, as he'd predicted. Carlie wished she could predict what was in store for them as a couple. If he didn't start picking up after himself, their co-habiting would be short-lived, and there definitely wouldn't be a wedding.

There was a dilemma involving Oscar. The second Larry was aware Carlie had taken in a dog, he was vaguely annoyed. His remark was, "Did you talk to the pediatrician about the germs involved with having a dog in the house?"

At first Carlie couldn't reply because she thought he was joking. Upon looking at his expression, she realized he was serious. She told him, "Yes, I did. It's all good." (Carlie would bring up the issue at Joey's next appointment with the pediatrician.)

Larry nodded but appeared to be thinking about something else. Carlie did not look forward to leaving Oscar home alone with Larry and the baby. Oscar had quickly become her friend, making her wonder how she ever got by not having a canine companion. His company was more enjoyable than moody Larry's.

The last thing Carlie wanted to do was come home from

work and find Oscar had "disappeared." She wouldn't put it past Larry to literally throw Oscar out the front door. Oscar would in turn run off in disgust, but Larry would claim he had no idea what happened to the dog. One thing Larry was good at was pleading ignorance. He probably did that one too many times at work, which contributed to why he lost his job.

Despite her misgivings, Carlie dared to trust Larry with Oscar. After all, Larry would be taking care of their baby while she was at work, and there was no greater responsibility than that. However, Carlie's mother was willing to be a substitute sitter if need be, although she did request twenty-four hours' notice.

About a month into this new live-in arrangement, Larry announced before he and Carlie went to bed, "I forgot to tell you, I have an interview tomorrow at eleven, on the west side of the valley."

"So you can't babysit Joey?"

"I can until ten. Then I'll be gone until twelve-thirty or one."

"I'll have Mom pick up Joey in the morning and just keep him until I get off work. Hopefully she'll agree to that because she told me she'd like some notice if she has to babysit." Carlie didn't mention her mother wanted an entire day's notice, as it would only give Larry more ammunition against her (Carlie's mother). Those two didn't like each other from the onset, and the situation was worsening.

"O.K. Whatever."

Just like that? Obviously since Larry had dutifully babysat for a month, he decided he had free rein to take off. Carlie was all for him having his own income again and helping out with household expenses, but she had a feeling he'd not only already given up on the idea of a home-based business but was using a job interview as an excuse to get out of the house. Her mother would say, "I told you so," when Carlie admitted she needed a babysitter again, already.

It was almost ten-thirty, so Carlie's mother was probably in bed. The last thing Carlie wanted to do was wake her up and tell her, her babysitting services were needed for the following day. Carlie would call her at 6:30 in the morning. Bonnie could be flexible with her work schedule—if she felt like it. Bonnie wasn't vindictive, but she so disliked Larry, anything was possible.

Bonnie got a phone call from her daughter at six-thirty this morning, asking if she, Bonnie, was available to babysit Joey later that morning. Carlie had been warned to give plenty of notice. As it was, Larry was supposed to stay home for the day with the baby, but he obviously decided he'd had enough of sitting around in his sweatpants, watching porn on the Internet. Bonnie hated to assume he did that, but why should she think he was doing something worthwhile, given the fact she couldn't stand him anyway? The number one reason Bonnie did not like Larry had to do with how poorly he treated Carlie. Worse, Carlie accepted his treatment of her as "normal." Since Melvin, Carlie's father, left before Carlie could notice how rude he could be to Bonnie, it was impossible that had anything to do with her daughter's outlook (at least as far as Bonnie was concerned). One more thing: Carlie was totally naive in regard to her assessment of people, particularly one Larry Gremble. (His physical attractiveness got in the way of any objectiveness on Carlie's part.)

"I'll be over as soon as I can," Bonnie said. "If you need to leave for work, go ahead. Larry can wait to take off until I get there."

"I'll tell him," Carlie said. "Thank you, Mom. I love you."

"I love you too," Bonnie said. She wanted to be helpful, which was why she would pick up Joey, versus making Carlie drop him off.

Larry sure didn't like the look his future (maybe) mother-in-law gave him before he left for his job interview across the valley. He was so mad at her he wanted to kick the dog on the way out the door and wanted "Mom" to see him do it. He had the opportunity because the stupid animal was right in the way. However, it must have guessed Larry's intentions because it sure as hell got out of the way fast enough! It was so impressive he had to chuckle, which really pissed off Carlie's mother. She'd already witnessed what might have transpired but didn't bother scolding him, which was a huge surprise. Maybe she was distracted, holding Joey. Plainly she was enamored with her grandchild. Otherwise Larry would have turned around and kicked her! That was a joke—sort of. What got him the most pissed was she showed up here at Carlie's house and acted like she owned the place. What about Larry? He happened to be living here with Carlie, and the kid in question was his. What more did the old bitty need from him for credentials, as far as getting some respect?

The real question was, why did Carlie have a *&#@ dog? Supposedly it would have been dumped somewhere or euthanized if Carlie hadn't taken it in for a friend or neighbor, two ridiculous lies told to her, both of which she evidently believed. If Larry had known how gullible Carlie was, he would have told her to abort her baby because it would be born with no arms or legs. Also, her life would be in danger if she carried the baby to term.

On second thought, Larry would have only used the former "threat," as Carlie would have been willing to die to save her baby. He never would have described her as matronly until seeing her with Joey. She was a great mom, damn it! Rather than be proud of as much, Larry was resentful, simultaneously aware his sentiment was fucked up!

Anyway, Bonnie said she was going to take Joey home with her, as she had a crib there (the one left over from her two kids). However, it didn't appear she was planning to leave and instead carried Joey back toward the bedrooms.

After the job interview, Joey considered stopping someplace and having a beer, although he wasn't a drinker. His kid was in good hands, so why not take his time going home?

Amy Kristoff

As it was, he'd dutifully babysat his son for the past month (for him that was like eternity). With his looks, even though he was no spring chicken, he deserved to go out and be seen, maybe even get a date. If Carlie didn't approve, too bad!

Ever since Carlie left for work she'd been worried about the goings on at home, specifically the interaction between her mother and Larry, with Carlie's son and her dog in the middle. The second Carlie got to her desk, she tried calling Larry on his cell phone, but there was no answer. Rather than text him, she called her mother's cell phone. Again, there was no answer. Whatever was going on was between them, and hopefully they left Joey and Oscar out of it.

The best thing Carlie did was settle down to work and not obsess over what was going on at home. Meanwhile, who stopped by Emerald Desert Inn but the owner, Jay Somerfield, whom Carlie had never met. If Melissa was still a hostess at the restaurant, she would have let Carlie know Mr. Somerfield was making an appearance. He had never stopped here since Carlie was employed at the hotel. Carlie was always in the dark about goings on around here, so this was definitely a surprise. But she claimed to like surprises, didn't she?

One look at Mr. Somerfield and Carlie immediately wondered if he was married. Tall, sandy-blond hair, weathered face, chiseled features, he was so not her type. Then again, Carlie didn't have a type. Besides, she actually felt something here. In other words, she finally knew what it was like to be looked at with adoration (besides having her dog, Oscar, look at her like that).

The immediate morale boost compelled Carlie to reconsider what she felt when she was with her baby's daddy. Call her impulsive, but she was already prepared to jump ship from her relationship with Larry and move on.

MORE DOGS AND THEIR TWISTED TALES–
AND ONE CAT STORY

"Honey, come in the house," Jay implored his new wife, Carlie. She was on the widow's walk outside the master bedroom of the Mediterranean-style house they'd just moved into, on the south side of Camelback Mountain, not all the way up but close. It was bedtime, so she was wearing a long, white silk robe and nightgown, which should have made her noticeable. He hung back from the French doors, "afraid" he wouldn't see her. Both the privacy and the view were definitely at a premium. In the past week Carlie had taken to spending more and more time gazing at the stars before going to bed. In the meantime she had to put her dog Oscar in the care of her mother, who willingly took him because she'd complained about being lonely. However, that wasn't why Carlie had turned the dog over to her mother. The problem was the dog had suddenly started barking at Jay for no reason (so it appeared to Carlie) and wouldn't shut up. Jay knew exactly what was going on but pretended to be as clueless as his wife. It was all he could do to "save face."

No dog-person was Jay, but he understood the significance of having a pet. That was more than could have been said for Carlie's ex-boyfriend, her baby's father, who got dumped for that reason, among others. Jay was willing to adopt her son Joey, but that was not a sure thing because of all the legal issues. Meanwhile, the kid's father acted like he wanted nothing to do with his own son. At least Jay's heart was in the right place. (Jay took every possible opportunity to promote himself, despite the circumstances.)

This five-thousand square-foot gem was a tenth anniversary gift to Jay's first wife Mimi, but she died in a tragic accident back in L.A. before ever seeing the house. While grieving, Jay had remained in L.A. for the most part. He'd intended for Mimi and himself to make this place their main residence, as he had more business interests in Arizona than California at this point. He was in fact trying to sell his house in L.A. and would possibly later buy a small condominium there.

Amy Kristoff

Carlie quit her job at Emerald Desert Inn and stayed home with her baby, so she was given the responsibility of doing the decorating. She seemed to enjoy the task, and her mother stopped by daily to visit. Mrs. Jones had tried once to bring Oscar to visit as well, but he became so agitated upon arrival, it was necessary to take him back to her house. Jay wasn't home when that happened, but the dog must have anticipated the possible appearance of "the dreaded Jay" at any moment.

Love at first sight? Jay felt it in aces and spades upon first laying eyes on Carlie Jones. The last thing he'd expected was to fall in love again after losing his first wife. He wasn't a guy who thought he had much luck on his side, thanks to an extremely unfortunate mishap of his own, a decade and a half ago. It'd taken years of adjustment, but he'd tried to not let his guard down completely. Unfortunately he couldn't seem to learn his lesson! That was how Carlie's dog "caught him without his face" and wouldn't drop the issue. It wasn't Jay's fault he didn't have his realistic-looking latex mask on when the dog saw him. No one else had been home at the time. The problem was he hadn't been around a dog since he was a kid, and that was long before his face was permanently disfigured by a disgruntled employee at a hotel Jay used to own in L.A. The guy had been terminated for stealing yet no criminal charges were filed, as part of "the deal." Talk about being ungrateful to your boss. Jay used to be extraordinarily handsome, if he did say so, himself. Nowadays he pretended to be so.

It had been barely a year since Mimi passed away, and initially Larry had felt guilty for being so attracted to Carlie, who vaguely resembled Mimi. Carlie was so entirely lacking in pretense, it was impossible not to want to get to know her.

Carlie hadn't yet responded to Jay's request she come back in the house. He'd been so lost in thought he'd lost track of time. Lately he'd been super-distracted, but that was no excuse.

Finally Jay went up to the French doors leading to the widow's walk. There was a full-length mirror to Jay's right, on the walk-in closet door. Catching a glimpse of his face (or lack thereof), he was made aware of why Carlie hadn't come back inside—and why there was no trace of her.

That was two wives in short order. At least the first one lasted as long as she did. Carlie's dog had provided a good warning he was getting forgetful about keeping his lack of a face, a secret. Maybe it was time to get a cat and resign himself to being a widower. In the meantime, Jay had to call 9-1-1. Better put his mask on first.

An Apparition and a Pleasant Surprise

It had been Lucy Chase's dream for years to have her own dog grooming business, first and foremost so she would no longer have to work for anyone. She was aware that came with one-hundred percent responsibility for every aspect of her dog grooming establishment, including taking care of a client's dog if the owner failed to pick his or her pet up at closing time, five p.m.

Coincidentally Lucy had to put her twelve-year-old Beagle-mix to sleep shortly before she had a client fail to pick up her dog at the end of the day he was groomed. It turned out the woman, Ms. Regina Stable, had a fatal heart attack. Meanwhile, her mother delivered the news of her daughter's passing, the following morning. At least, Lucy thought it was Ms. Stable's mother.

Ms. Stable brought her dog, Percy, a Shih Tzu, to "The Canine Clipper," on a drizzly Monday morning in early March. Being Northwest Indiana, it just as easily could have been snowing. The town of Crown Point's growing popularity allowed Lucy to hang her shingle and have plenty of business. Also, the place of business was on Grant, a busy street. The former business in this thousand square-foot space was also for a dog groomer. Lucy couldn't imagine letting her business fail, unless perhaps she simply wasn't very good at it. Grooming dogs was all Lucy was interested in doing and liked to think she was pretty capable. A failed marriage in her late twenties soured her on any sort of cohabitation, and she'd never wanted kids. At fifty, this was as close to a perfect life as she could get, aside from having recently lost her beloved companion, Billie.

The lease-to-own rate was reasonable, considering it was in a newer building, on the edge of a large industrial complex. There was just enough space for a reception area, where there were also some collars and leashes on display, as well as several kinds of brushes and shampoos, to keep your dog "clean between appointments."

The remainder of the space was taken up by the work and bathing area. In the far back there were eight kennels for dogs waiting to be picked up. Lucy doubted she would ever be so busy a need for all the kennels would be necessary. The individual who originally had the place lost it because of using her finances to pay medical bills (versus paying her lease). Later the building was purchased by some investors, and Lucy was leasing the property from them, with the hope of purchasing it outright.

It never occurred to Lucy the responsibility of taking care of a client's dog overnight, would eventually take place. Her business had been operating about a year and a half, which should have given her enough time to be prepared "for anything" (within reason).

Ms. Stable had brought Percy to The Canine Clipper at precisely nine in the morning on that fateful day. She was punctual to the extreme and expected her dog to be ready at a specific time. Lucy had groomed Percy eighteen times, and only once did she not yet have him quite ready when Ms. Stable returned to pick him up. Her withering look said it all, and Lucy was never "unprepared," again.

The agreed-upon time for Percy to be ready was ten-thirty on this particular day. Usually Lucy was given until eleven. Since it was cold and drizzly, Lucy wanted to make sure Percy was completely dry before letting him leave. She would have to spend some time using a blow-dryer on him, which she hated doing. What dog liked the sound of one of those?

Percy was ready at exactly ten-thirty; he even had a blue

silk bow on top of his head. However, his owner was a no-show. Lucy was silently fuming. However, she didn't have time to dwell on her anger because her next appointment breezed in the door, which was a huge relief. Meanwhile, she put Percy in one of the kennels, and he in turn had a puzzled-looking expression, aware how obsessed his owner was about timeliness.

The next appointment was for another Shih Tzu, Candy, owned by Mrs. Kern, who was known to sit and wait while her "baby" was bathed and groomed. Lucy didn't have a problem with that, other than the fact it made her feel like she needed to invest in a television set for her small reception area. Fortunately Mrs. Kern had thus far been content to read a book she'd brought with her. (This was Candy's fourth grooming appointment.)

On this occasion, Mrs. Kern said she was dropping off Candy, and she had a "mani-pedi appointment." Her phone would be off because her manicurist got mad at her when she answered calls, so she planned on returning in a couple hours; therefore, Lucy didn't have to call her when Candy was ready. Nonetheless, Lucy made sure to confirm Mrs. Kern's cell phone number "just in case." Fortunately Mrs. Kern didn't look at Lucy like she was weird before making her departure.

Candy was a breeze to groom and bathe, so Lucy had her finished, including putting a hot pink bow on her head, long before Mrs. Kern was due to return from her manicurist appointment. Lucy was even interrupted twice because of clients wanting to make grooming appointments, both of them having never before visited her business.

Eleven forty-five and there was no sign of Percy's owner. Lucy placed Candy in a kennel across from him, so they could look at each other and keep one another company. Right after doing so, her phone rang again. Surely that was Ms. Stable, explaining her whereabouts. Instead, it was a solicitor. Usually Lucy managed to be courteous toward solicitors, but she couldn't help being curt. That was a sub-conscious indication it was going to be a long, unpredictable day. She considered calling Ms. Stable's cell phone, just to tell her anxious-looking Percy was ready to be picked up, but she decided to wait a little longer. That was the only number Lucy had on file to call because Ms. Stable didn't give her any other options. Typically Lucy required an alternative/emergency number, but for some reason she didn't press the issue with Ms. Stable.

In came the third appointment of the day, Mrs. Thomas' Susie, a miniature Schnauzer. It would be the dog's second visit. Last time, Mrs. Thomas gave Lucy a ten-dollar cash tip, which was the first tip Lucy had ever received since she opened her business. If the tips from Mrs. Thomas continued and increased incrementally, that was fine with Lucy.

Once Susie was finished, Lucy called Mrs. Thomas to tell her. Mrs. Thomas said, "Great. I happen to be pulling into the parking lot right now. I had something come up and was hoping she would be ready about now. See you in a sec." Lucy hated to be greedy, but she wondered if she would get more of a tip this time, thanks to her efficiency.

Thanks to her greediness, Lucy didn't get a tip at all! It was plain Mrs. Thomas was in a hurry, so perhaps Lucy would receive a tip next time. Or maybe it was an every-other-visit kind of thing.

Whatever the case, Lucy wished Ms. Stable would come pick up Percy. Meanwhile, Mrs. Kern showed up for Candy, leaving Percy alone in the kennel area. He looked so forlorn Lucy almost cried. It didn't help she had yet to get over losing Billie. It had been especially difficult for Lucy because she was not only a confirmed dog-person, she lived alone. As much as she craved having companionship again, she didn't feel "ready" to start over with another dog. Obviously she was grieving her loss and needed more time. Having no immediate family in the area contributed to her feeling of isolation, which ironically compelled her to crave more of the same when she was feeling down.

It was past lunch time for Lucy, so she took a quick break and had a granola bar. To drink she had a soda. Was that being hypocritical? Even though she had a small refrigerator here, rarely did she bother to stock it with anything.

Lucy's phone rang. That had to be Ms. Stable, letting Lucy know she was on her way to pick up Percy. Instead, it was a woman named Lynn Land, who needed her standard poodle groomed "as soon as possible." Lucy told her tomorrow at nine was still available. Ms. Land said she and Romeo would be there then, equipped with specific instructions as to how he needed to be groomed.

After penciling in Romeo for nine a.m., Lucy decided she had enough appointments for the following day, as the next ones were at eleven, noon, one, two-thirty, and four. It would be a busy day. This one was slower, but she didn't mind. The last thing she wanted to do was get sick of doing what she loved. She'd vowed when she started this business, she'd pace herself. Having peace of mind was more important than making a lot of money (but that wasn't the worst thing).

Enough was enough. Lucy finally called Ms. Stable's cell phone. She didn't answer, so when it went to voicemail, Lucy left the following message: "Hello, this is Lucy from The Canine Clipper. I just wanted to let you know Percy was ready at ten-thirty, as you'd requested. We'll be looking forward to seeing you soon. Bye."

Although it wasn't the worst thing if Ms. Stable didn't show up for Percy, Lucy had a feeling of doom, of all things. At the very least, if Percy was stuck here overnight, it would be an unprecedented situation.

It was five-thirty. Percy had to be super-anxious by this time, although he was doing an amazing job of holding up, despite undoubtedly wondering what the flip was going on. He wasn't Lucy's dog, so there was little she could do to reassure him (such as take him home with her). Admittedly Lucy was entirely unprepared for this situation, so Percy would have to be content with a couple biscuits for dinner. Tomorrow morning she would bring the rest of the bag of Billie's food. In the meantime, maybe Ms. Stable would call so she could pick her dog up after hours. Lucy would be happy to come back here tonight, so she would make sure her phone was on.

The stress of wondering if/when Ms. Stable would return to claim her dog must have exhausted Lucy because she fell asleep in her navy leather recliner in the den, the book she'd been reading having fallen on the wood floor. It was a pretty large hardcover, and not even the sound of it hitting the floor, awoke her. Lucy finally stumbled into bed at three a.m. Before going to sleep, she thought of Percy at The Canine Clipper and felt terrible for him. Then she felt guilty for failing to even consider the well-being of Percy's mistress, Ms. Stable.

Lucy's "selfishness" caused her to have insomnia until about an hour before she needed to get up, seven a.m. Not surprisingly she was still very tired when the alarm clock went off. However, she felt an adrenaline rush upon remembering Percy was waiting for her. Or she expected as much.

Hurriedly Lucy took a shower and went to The Canine Clipper. Typically she entered via the front door (versus the back). Percy started loudly yipping as soon as she turned the key in the glass entryway door. Lucy was so relieved he was apparently O.K., she almost cried.

Lucy greeted Percy face-to-face, and as much as she wanted to take him for a walk outside, doing so wasn't worth the risk. Cleaning the cage would have to suffice. Not too surprisingly, Percy wanted nothing to do with the dry food Lucy had brought him.

Since the shop wasn't open yet, Lucy had locked the front door after she'd entered. From the kennel area, a knock could be heard on that very door. Percy was oblivious to as much and was staring at her, as if trying to tell her he wanted out of this place. It seemed like just about any dog responded to the sound of someone knocking, no matter where the dog might be, so that was the first thing that seemed strange. It wasn't like he was deaf.

As the knocking continued, Lucy became completely creeped-out and didn't want to see who was out there on this chilly morning, the sun barely having risen. Nonetheless, Lucy went to the reception area, where she could see who was at the door: a short, petite, older woman wearing a bulky-looking, dark-colored car coat and a dark-colored scarf on her head, some tufts of gray hair sticking out. No longer was Lucy "creeped-out," but she remained somewhat wary.

Lucy unlocked the door and greeted the woman: "Good morning. I'm Lucy. Can I help you?"

"I'm Regina Stable's mother, Charlotte," the woman replied. "Her dog Percy was left here overnight because she died! She had a heart attack the moment she sat down at her desk at the legal firm where she worked. She drove herself into the ground with all her obsessions! She got those from me. You'd probably find this too coincidental, but I actually had a grooming business here. I lost it way too soon to medical bills I had to pay. I kept thinking I'd have enough for the lease payments, but business was never that great, not that I wasn't making decent money. Then I got really sick and di...Anyway, I'm not here to drag you down with my sorrows, just tell you to take good care of Percy, with Regina's blessing!"

Lucy leaned to shake Mrs. Stable's hand, only to find nothing but space. A loud bark from Percy brought Lucy back to reality and back inside, to take care of "her new dog."

The Walk with Mort

What a hell-day at work. Nothing was so horrible it was life-changing for the worse, but Jill always did have a bit of a poor-me attitude. However, even she was aware there was nothing "poor" about her circumstances. She was still relatively "young" (forty) and was above-average in the looks department (and holding up well). She also had a rewarding job, emotionally more than financially. The job was exasperating at times, such as today, but it didn't take much to set her off (only her mother knew that, as well as a couple ex-boyfriends who'd crossed the line one too many times).

Although Jill had never married nor had kids, she'd had a number of fulfilling relationships. Only recently had she been "alone," although that wasn't quite the case because her on-off-on boyfriend, Chet, couldn't seem to say good-bye. And she couldn't say bye to him either, despite the fact he was no longer exclusively dating her, which would otherwise annoy her. What was up? Maybe it had to do with the fact all she had for company was her eight-year-old black Labrador, Mort. He was named for her deceased father, Morton. Jill had been a Daddy's girl, to the point it appeared to irritate her mother, Andrea. Jill used to think it was funny, even as she looked back on her youth. Lately, however, she reflected on her past and became angry with her mother, even going so far as to blame her for how comparatively eccentric she (Jill) was. Her mother was in fact alive and well, but the two had a strained relationship, thanks to Jill's many resentments. Her mother would attempt to patch things up by inviting Jill

93

to lunch or go shopping, but Jill always had an excuse to say no.

Fortunately Jill was driving away from her place of work, where she'd felt like fleeing way before quitting time. She hesitated explaining where she was employed and what happened. With her luck she'd be fired and sued as a result. Maybe she was simply having more and more difficulty tolerating stupidity in people. Or perhaps she could no longer put up with her own stupidity. Either way, Jill was in desperate need of an attitude adjustment before work tomorrow morning.

One way for Jill to alleviate stress was to take a walk with Mort after work. He too appeared to enjoy the walks around the Scottsdale, Arizona neighborhood where they resided in a three-bedroom, adobe-style house. Even Chet occasionally accompanied them, should he stop by in time after getting off work. His position at a bank required him to stay later than Jill did at her job, so sometimes she and Mort took a second walk, just so Chet could accompany them. Someone was dedicated in all this. Suffice to mention, Chet didn't just leave again after the walk. He'd stay for dinner and "something more," and this was the case after they'd technically broken up—or at least had mutually agreed it wasn't necessary to remain exclusive. Meanwhile, she had yet to meet anyone new.

It must be mentioned Jill had in fact invited Chet to live with her, but the invite turned out to be a mistake. He couldn't wait to become a slovenly bum who expected Jill to pick up after him and cook dinner every evening. She had broken up with guys because of their sloppiness, yet they were neater than him!

During the time the three of them lived together, Chet was known to take Mort on a walk and even took him to the nearby dog park on a couple of occasions. Jill had kept her concern about the latter to herself, as she didn't want to hear Chet telling her to "loosen up and quit being so worried about everything." For a guy who worked in the banking world, one would have thought he was the tense, high-strung one.

Having mentioned the hell-day Jill had at work, she'd leave out the details but would mention she did take a short detour on the way home, stopping at a new outdoor shopping center that recently opened in place of several ramshackle stucco houses that had been torn down.

"La Plaza Bonita" shopping mall included a make-up/beauty store that Jill had glommed onto upon her first stop in it a week ago, "Glam R." It was the last store to open, after "Nina's," a terrific women's wear boutique Jill had immediately taken a liking to as well. Another place she liked was "Jo-Jo's," a coffee and pastry hangout she typically saved for the weekend. Chet and she in fact went there yesterday, around eleven. He'd spent the night and after a late start and a walk with Mort (just the two of them), Jill and he had gone to Jo-Jo's for a bite to eat and some en plein air people watching. The day couldn't have been more perfect. After Chet had left, having driven to Jo-Jo's separately, Jill had wondered if they'd ever see one another again. What of it? Since they'd agreed not to be a couple, his visits could cease at any time.

A mere day later and the vibe was entirely different. Call her crazy, but Jill was convinced the day seemed "off." And that vibe continued when Jill stepped inside her house via the side door leading from the two-vehicle carport to the kitchen. As usual Mort was right inside the doorway to greet her, but on this occasion he proceeded to snarl and growl, the fur on his back standing on end!

"Mort!" Jill cried. "What's the matter with you? You're supposed to be happy to see me."

Jill's voice appeared to awaken Mort to reality, at least somewhat, as he stopped growling. However, he kept snarling while slowly backing up. He refused to turn around and was determined to keep making eye contact with her. She looked right back at him, scared shitless—like him?

By this time Jill's heart was beating wildly, not only out of fear but anger. How could her reliable (up until now) companion do this to her? All she'd wanted was take Mort for a walk, and he'd backed out of the kitchen and was probably hiding behind the living room sofa, where he liked to go, on the rare occasion it stormed. Since doing that as good as told her he didn't want to take a walk with her, she'd go by herself.

Jill hurried into her bedroom and quickly changed into comfortable walking attire, not even glancing in a mirror before going back outside. If Mort made a mess on the slate-tiled floor that was throughout the house, so be it. She'd always let him have the run of the place, and he had yet to have an accident.

It almost seemed like Jill needed a "back-up dog" for occasions such as this. At the same time, a dog wasn't something you had in multiples, just like a boyfriend. Maybe she was too pragmatic.

Jill did not mind living alone but she HAD TO HAVE A DOG. That meant he/she was always game for anything. Jill would make do for the time being by going on a walk alone, but she was not about to let this become a habit, nor did she intend to stay home as a show of solidarity for Mort. She was so anxious she was ready to jump out of her skin, so a walk was exactly what she needed. There was no use in expecting a visit from Chet, as he'd already done the unexpected by spending most of the weekend with her (and Mort). Jill had reminded herself innumerable times "anytime could be the last," when Chet might come over. Before leaving her, he never said, "I'll see you later" or whatever. There was usually a quick kiss good-bye initiated by him and that was it. In a way, Jill liked the arbitrary facet of their "new" (open) relationship, even though she wasn't seeing anyone else.

After taking one last look behind the sofa to confirm Mort was sitting behind it like he was glued to the floor, Jill departed for a walk. She kept telling herself to think positive thoughts, such as considering the wonders the new "day cream" she'd just purchased at Glam R. would do for her face, not that she didn't look good for her age. She'd bought a small jar (it was super expensive), and she'd had a free sample applied right at the store! Purchasing the "night cream" would require some saving up. (She only paid cash for "luxury" items.) Jill was amazed the aesthetician was so generous. Bella was the woman's name, and she had been very pleasant. She'd explained her background was more extensive than it would appear, selling make-up and lotions. Naturally Jill was very impressed and in turn willing to believe anything Bella said. Besides, she was extraordinarily attractive and her skin was flawless, two great selling points for a store like this.

Bella had offered to give Jill a free make-up session, but Jill told her maybe another time. The way Mort reacted upon seeing Jill, one would have thought Jill did have a make-up session, and Bella went overboard with the cosmetics. Typically Jill wore a minimal amount of make-up for every-day, so Mort would have been shocked to see his mistress "all made up."

Jill almost left for her walk, forgetting her phone. Her friend Patty was going to text her when she knew the diagnosis of her daughter Tina's sore throat. She was six and had missed school because she was so miserable (and it was feared she might be contagious). Patty was only able to get her in for a late afternoon appointment. Hopefully it was nothing serious.

At the end of her driveway Jill turned right and walked south on 62nd Street until reaching Azul Lane. She had yet to see anyone outside, despite the perfect weather. Not even a vehicle had passed by. One reason she liked this part of Scottsdale, known as "Arcadia," was the peacefulness yet the closeness to many amenities. If she took Azul and circled back around it would barely be a block. Hopefully Mort would miss her if she was gone a few extra minutes, so she continued walking south to Lafayette Boulevard, which was wide, flat and had a generous bicycle lane on either side. It was definitely busier than any side streets, and Lafayette was in fact usually part of one of the routes she took with Mort.

Reaching the corner of 62nd and Lafayette, Jill turned left, intending to walk east until she came to 63rd. There she'd head north and eventually west, toward home. However, she wouldn't use Azul Lane because it didn't go straight through between 62nd and 63rd. Instead she'd use Verde Way.

A black Ford Expedition approached as Jill walked in the bicycle lane on Lafayette into traffic. The SUV had tinted windows, so it was impossible to confirm if the driver looked at her, but the vehicle noticeably slowed down when it passed by.

Not more than five seconds later a white Chevrolet Suburban approached, and Jill could see the long-haired blonde behind the wheel just fine. The woman didn't slow her Suburban as much as the Expedition driver did, but it was easy to see her expression of shock. Meanwhile Jill was ready to laugh, erroneously thinking the woman was staring at her because of looking "old."

About fifty yards before Jill reached 63rd, a male bicyclist approached, wearing a colorful, short-sleeved Spandex shirt, black spandex shorts, a black helmet and mirrored sunglasses. He appeared intent upon avoiding any debris that might be in the roadway, until he sharply turned his bicycle, to pass Jill on his right. She had been walking close to the curb, so evidently he hadn't seen her. When he finally did he muttered, "Oh my God."

Clearly the cyclist was talking to himself, so Jill didn't bother calling him out, such as asking him, "What's wrong, mister?" Instead she walked faster, telling herself she was only doing so to burn more calories. Truthfully she just wanted to get the walk she'd looked forward to, over with.

On 63rd, Jill was making good time. Perhaps her brisk

walking pace was what caused the woman in a white stucco bungalow with a single-vehicle carport to pause while unloading groceries from the trunk of a white Ford Focus. She looked over her shoulder at Jill, shook her head, and quickly took her bags of grocery purchases into the house.

Finally it dawned on Jill to be concerned about her appearance. Then Chet called. After Jill answered, he asked her, "What's wrong? You sound weird."

"I'm on a walk and I feel weird. Or I didn't until I started wondering what I look like because everyone's staring at me."

"You always worry about what people think when they look at you. I wish you'd get over that."

"No, this is something else," Jill declared, but there was so much more she wanted to say, including the issue with Mort.

"I was going to have dinner with an acquaintance, but I cancelled because I'd rather be with you. How about another go of it, us living together? The weekend was fantastic, and I know you enjoyed yourself, Jill. What can I do to convince you?"

Just as Jill started to say, "Nothing! We're done, you slob!" the tips of her fingers brushed her face as she held her phone. It felt like there were porcupine quills protruding from her skin, from around her nose, outward. How come she didn't feel any pain? Was her face numb? "Jill, are you there?" Chet asked, sounding concerned. That was just it. He only sounded that way. One of his "other lays" (Jill's description) was busy tonight, despite his contention he was having dinner with "an acquaintance." Sadly, if it didn't feel as if Jill had quills bursting through the skin on her face, she would have fallen for Chet's charms once again and invited him over.

Finally Jill said, "I'm here. I can't talk anymore right now. I'll call you later maybe."

"Wait, Jill," Chet implored. "Please don't hang up. I know you were never keen on me seeing other women, but you were free to go out with other guys. I point this out because I feel like you're punishing me out of jealousy."

"Chet, I cannot talk now, I have too much going on," Jill told him, hoping he got the hint. Then she said bye and ended the call.

Jill tried to remain calm but it was nearly impossible. She told herself to walk home and look in a mirror before letting herself totally freak out.

Chet Morgenstern's girlfriend, Jill, deserved to be angry with him because of his ongoing ambivalence toward her, which caused him to be a selfish pig. That was his justification for being a lazy slob when she'd generously invited him to move in with her. He'd tested her love for him to the limit, and he blew his welcome.

This time around, Chet wouldn't take Jill for granted and would be neat (so he said). He was driving to her house to make his plea face-to-face, knowing she found him extremely irresistible. Besides, her dog, Mort, liked him, so Chet unequivocally deserved another chance. He was supposed to have met a gal for dinner, but she'd cancelled at the last minute, and he had a feeling it had to do with the fact she was only twenty-one to his forty-two and she did the math.

Jill was a bit eccentric, but it wasn't like she was outright crazy or dangerous in any way. If she was "crazy" he loved her all the more, and if he was "crazy" too, so be it. In other words he loved her. He wished he would have told her as much long ago and would have quit playing the field right under her nose, per her "O.K." Her worst fault was acting like her job was so stressful and demanding, dramatizing every element of being employed as: a kindergarten teacher! The fact Jill never had kids of her own (nor wanted any) was evidently what made for the high drama. At the same time, she was supposedly very popular with her young students, so that should have said it all. If nothing else she put up a good front.

MORE DOGS AND THEIR TWISTED TALES–
AND ONE CAT STORY

Meanwhile, Chet intended to bare his feelings to Jill, and he was working up the nerve on his way to her house. Upon reaching the driveway, he was so agitated he almost left again. After all, she practically hung up on him, as she was (finally) playing hard to get. This was a new one, and it really turned him on.

Rather than park his white Jeep Cherokee next to her white Kia Soul, underneath the carport, Chet parked behind her vehicle. That way if she stormed out of the house to get away from him, it would have to be on foot—and he'd follow her, making his case.

Chet knocked on the front door and waited. He'd returned the key Jill had given him, so he was completely at her mercy. He briefly looked around, wondering if she hadn't yet returned from her walk. What about Mort? How come she didn't make any mention of him? He was like the ultimate love of her life, so it was completely unlike her not to have mentioned something about the dog.

From the side door, Chet heard Jill say, "I'm over here, Chet. Why don't you come back over to the carport and come in the kitchen?"

Chet's intuition told him to leave. At the same time, men weren't supposed to have intuition. Or were they were too stubborn to heed it?

Andrea Meyers was proud of the fact she'd gone the "tough love" route with her only child, Jill. Already forty, Jill was still a bit of a brat in Andrea's eyes, but she'd taken a step back, vowing to be less critical of the "monster" she'd created. That sounded like overkill, but at times it appeared to be accurate. Nonetheless, Andrea wanted to bury the hatchet with her daughter. Andrea's best friend since grade school, Cheryl, was recently diagnosed with an illness and was told she only had six months to live, which was supposedly an optimistic prediction. Having heard as much, Andrea suddenly realized how precious time was. (Losing her husband when their daughter was only ten, didn't do it.) Andrea was even willing to skip a stop at a new make-up/beauty store on her way, one she had yet to visit. For how expensive the department store anti-aging creams were, she was willing to try someplace else's, although it was probably pricey there, too.

The truth of the matter was Andrea resented the fact Jill "got along" with her father, Mort, better than his wife got along with him. An admitted "Daddy's girl" growing up, Andrea was envious of her daughter having enjoyed the same. It was entirely possible Jill hated Andrea for that alone, but again, it was time for bygones to be bygones. At least it was worth a try.

Anyway, Andrea drove to her daughter's house and parked her red Chevy Cruze on the left side of the driveway, next to a white Jeep Cherokee, which was parked behind Jill's Kia. Andrea wasn't even remotely up-to-date on what was going on in her daughter's personal life, and it was no secret Jill didn't like living alone. She claimed her dog, Mort, provided ample companionship, but she was basically lost without a boyfriend. Andrea didn't like being single, but she couldn't even begin to replicate the love she'd shared with her husband. The memory of him had become a form of company, as weird as that sounded.

Andrea exited her car and debated about going any further. How could she feel so much trepidation about paying an unannounced visit to her daughter? Andrea's "tough love" must not have worked, so she still had a spoiled brat on her hands. That was the only explanation for her feeling so intimidated.

"Hello, Mom. Come in," Jill said from the side doorway, although Andrea couldn't see her, not because of the shadow cast by the carport but the fact Jill remained inside.

"Jill?" Andrea said because her daughter sounded so different, so—calm and sweet? Even when Jill would deign to be polite, she never sounded like that.

MORE DOGS AND THEIR TWISTED TALES–
AND ONE CAT STORY

Not only did Jill not answer with what would have been typical for her in this situation (sarcasm), she didn't say anything! Worse, Andrea was compelled to leave immediately, fearful of her own daughter. Worse yet, she forced herself to enter the opened doorway that led to the kitchen. Jill was nowhere to be seen—at first. As soon as Andrea started to scream, Jill slammed the door.

Patty Wall texted her friend Jill to let her know Patty's daughter Tina was already better after taking the medicine she was prescribed. Patty started to type a joke about swilling the remainder herself, but lately Jill had been acting strangely and might not "see" the humor. Patty figured it had to do with the fact Jill's boyfriend, Chet, treated her like crap, coming and going as he pleased, which was stressing Jill out.

Jill never failed to text Patty back, even during the school day, when Jill was in the kindergarten class she taught. Jill had already mentioned a million times, the great weekend she'd had with that shit Chet, so maybe they were re-connecting in a big way, as in he'd finally proposed. Otherwise there was no explanation for Patty not having heard back from her friend, an hour-plus since sending the text update regarding Tina.

Patty would see Tina off to school tomorrow morning and then go to Jill's if she didn't contact Patty by then. If Jill was sick, she wouldn't dare go to work, nor would she be mad at Patty for just showing up.

Bugsby

Bugsby disappeared out of the fenced backyard. The weird part was he wasn't a digger and didn't dig under the fence so he could escape. Both gates were locked and no one had a key to the padlocks, including Bryant, Marsha's ex-husband. He did have a key to the house, but Marsha made him return it when he moved out, long before the divorce was finalized. Financially he had provided well for his family, but he kept cheating on Marsha (while denying it). Finally enough was enough. It was a tough decision for her because she still had feelings for him. One thing he came to hate about her was her obsession with fitness, yet he only found physically fit women, attractive.

As much as Marsha missed Bugsby, their daughter Mona was the one who was positively devastated. She was only ten, and she took the dog's disappearance personally. Marsha had gone jogging on the path along the canal near her Scottsdale, Arizona home and usually took Bugsby, especially if it wasn't yet completely light outside, such as this early January morning. On this particular day, however, she felt like running alone, so she left him in the fenced yard for the duration, never considering that within thirty minutes he would disappear. Meanwhile Mona slept through the apparent abduction and didn't ask about him until after sitting down at the kitchen table for breakfast and Bugsby was nowhere to be seen. The first question Mona had asked was, "Where's Bugsby?"

Marsha had attempted to sound calm, saying (but not believing it), "He must have gotten out of the yard while I was running."

"You didn't take him?"

"No, not this morning."

"Why not?"

"I just didn't, O.K.?" Marsha was ready to lose it. Her daughter seemed to enjoy being difficult whenever Marsha needed her to just lay off! "Hopefully he's running around the neighborhood and someone will recognize him." Although he had a rabies tag, he had no I. D. tag because something like this wasn't supposed to happen!

"Then what?" Mona asked, really pushing Marsha's buttons.

"Either they'll bring him here or take him to Paradise Animal Shelter since it's close," Marsha replied. "After I drop you off at school, I'll go see if he's there."

"What if he isn't?"

"Honey, let's worry about that when the time comes."

Rather than say anything else, Mona finally ate the cereal Marsha had just served her. As Marsha turned away, she caught her daughter giving her one of those exasperated looks that should have been a few years away. The divorce appeared to have accelerated everything in both their lives: Marsha looked like she had aged ten years (yet her body still looked fabulous, if she did say so herself); Mona acted like she was fifteen going on twenty and about ready to move out and live on her own.

Not so fast! Marsha received a very reasonable sum every month for child support. Bryant was not only done with Marsha, he didn't care about his kid, although he was never late in any payments, which some would have said meant more than anything.

While Mona was finishing her cereal, Marsha looked up "Paradise Animal Shelter" on her phone. It didn't open until ten, and that was the extent of her investigation of the place.

Marsha would have almost two hours to kill after she dropped off Mona at school. There was a yoga class she wanted to attend for a free trial at a new fitness center that just opened on Camelback Road. It was only a couple miles from home and on the way to Paradise Animal Shelter. She could take a cover-up or even a change of clothes with her and go straight to the shelter afterward. Bryant had no idea the monster he'd created in his ex-wife, insofar as her obsession with exercise and fitness. Not only that, he'd liked the fact she stayed home while he earned all the dough, so keeping fit became a job for Marsha, without her even being aware of as much. Nowadays, all she could do to stay afloat mentally was keep doing the same thing, especially since her ex financially supported it.

Marsha was never so relieved to drop Mona off at school. Usually she was sorry to do so, never looking forward to a day spent alone for the most part, save for Bugsby's company—and now Marsha didn't even have that. Maybe she needed to join so many exercise classes she'd not only satisfy her loneliness, she'd be too exhausted to complain about being lonely. Otherwise she needed to get a job, a thought that made her cringe. She hadn't worked at an actual place of employment since high school and was completely accustomed to the lifestyle she currently enjoyed, which included running errands, keeping the house clean and "working" to stay in shape. The divorce was final, and Bryant had a girlfriend, yet Marsha still thought he'd come running back to her if her ass was firm enough.

Rather than go to the free yoga class, Marsha decided to drive around the neighborhood, hoping Bugsby would materialize. After about an hour of that, she was so frustrated she started to cry. Her eyes were so tear-filled the only place to go was home and see if maybe Bugsby had returned.

No, he hadn't. Marsha waited there until Paradise Animal Shelter opened. Apparently Mona's anxiety about Bugsby was contagious, not that Marsha didn't have feelings for

Bugsby. Nonetheless, ever since Bryant physically left (before the divorce proceedings took place), Marsha felt like nothing was as important as having lost her husband's attention.

Paradise Animal Shelter was located in a spacious, adobe-style building on Lincoln Road, in what was formerly the Paradise Valley Post Office. Apparently mail inventory was down but not runaway and stray dogs and cats.

There was a large waiting area inside, a leftover from the building's life as a post office. Behind the counter there was a tall, big-boned woman with brunette hair pulled back. Marsha's initial impression before exchanging even one word with her was the woman was prone to something self-serving. The I.D. card read "Rhonda M." Having come here to hopefully retrieve Bugsby and nothing more, Marsha had failed to read the shelter's website, which would have told her what Rhonda's last name was, not that it would have been notable at a stressful time like this.

Marsha skipped any sort of greeting and told Rhonda, "My dog Bugsby, a Dalmatian, got out of the backyard early this morning, and I just wanted to have a quick look in the back to see if he's there."

"You don't need to do that," Rhonda stated, stone-faced. "The dog's not back there. If he had been picked up, I would have been told about it immediately, as the van driver is out and about right at this moment."

"Could I give you my phone number and e-mail in case you do find him?" Marsha asked, simultaneously aware she was making a request for naught. The woman's behavior was mind-blowing.

Amazingly enough, Rhonda managed to produce a piece of paper and a pen, thereby "allowing" Marsha to write down her contact information. While she was doing so, it was undeniable "Rhonda M." was trying to kill her with her stare.

Marsha exited Paradise Animal Shelter in tears. All she could think about was Mona, how her mother had just failed her and Bugsby too. What Marsha dreaded most was telling

Mona, "Bugsby's gone. Sorry." It wouldn't surprise Marsha if her daughter tried to run away! Marsha needed to remind her not to bother running away to Dad because he didn't want her.

After stopping at the supermarket to pick up a few items, Marsha would go home and clean the house. Then she'd take a midday run along the canal before showering and getting ready to pick up Mona from school. Suddenly all that activity sounded so depressing! As it was, despite burning thousands of calories, mainly for the sake of impressing Bryant, had it done any good?

Rhonda Martenowsky took her job as director of Paradise Animal Shelter, very seriously. That was to say she was extremely fair-minded when it came to dogs in particular. Whenever a stray with a collar was found roaming around the Scottsdale, Paradise Valley and Phoenix streets, she wanted to scream, "How the %$*# could any self-respecting dog owner allow his or her pet to get out of sight long enough to end up loose?"

Rhonda's one full-time assistant, Cory Rogers, was almost as dedicated as Rhonda, but she didn't have the nerve her boss did. To eliminate raising suspicion, Rhonda made sure to treat Cory very well, such as letting her drive the shelter's pick-up van home last evening, since Cory's car was in the shop. Coincidentally she picked up a runaway on her way to work around nine-fifteen. It was a neutered male Dalmatian, Rhonda's favorite breed! The dog had a collar with a current rabies tag but no identification. That was a good thing because Cory would have already contacted the dog's owner, and Rhonda would have totally lost out! Instead Cory placed the dog in a cordoned off area in the back, specifically for ones like him. Meanwhile, the owner just showed up, but Rhonda managed to shoo her away. That was only possible because Cory had left again, having answered an anonymous call about a "German Shepherd type" that was darting in and out of traffic at Lincoln Road and Tatum Boulevard. Cory would have to clean the cages upon her return.

Rhonda went in the back to get acquainted with her new dog. After all, she hadn't had a dog of her own for awhile, and the Dalmatian was exactly what she wanted. Her actions were totally justified in Rhonda's mind, and the first order of business was to change his name from Bugsby to something more dignified.

Despite Rhonda's own rule, someone had to be at the front of the shelter during business hours, NO EXCEPTIONS, she was in the back petting her new dog, leaving the counter unattended. Barely had she spent any time with him when she heard a woman's voice in the front, saying, "Is anyone here? Hello?"

Rolling her eyes, Rhonda went to the counter to greet the tall, somewhat pretty (but she appeared very stressed) woman standing there, a blue leash in hand. She had her hopes up, anyway. She then asked if a male German Shepherd mix had been turned in, one with a red collar and rabies tag?

Rhonda told her, "My assistant got a call about a 'German Shepherd type' at Lincoln and Tatum, and she left to pick him up. That might be the dog you're inquiring about." Never was Rhonda so looking forward to the volunteers showing up around noon. Then Rhonda could take a long lunch break and take her new dog home with her (under the auspice of returning him to his owner). Meanwhile, Rhonda would send Cory off to pick up lunch for herself and everyone else—the tab on Rhonda. Cory definitely deserved a free lunch, having delivered to her boss, the dog of her dreams.

"Do you think you could call her and see if she got him?" the woman wanted to know.

"If she's busy trying to catch him, I doubt she's going to answer her phone," Rhonda replied, displaying her typically uncooperative attitude. Having gotten a good look at the woman's manicure, Rhonda's sympathy for her in any capacity was nonexistent.

Fortunately Rhonda's remark was enough to get the woman to leave, muttering as she made her departure.

Rhonda was smiling but not because of what she did. She was thinking of her new dog and could hardly wait to take him home. She wished Cory would come back soon and quit wasting her time trying to wrangle a dog someone obviously didn't really care about. Rhonda was worried about her and didn't want her to get hit by a car while trying to do her job. She was a valued employee!

The most difficult thing Bryant Morrow ever did wasn't divorce his wife but steal the family dog from the backyard of what was technically his house (he had to make the payments on it as part of the divorce agreement). Bryant then took the dog and dumped him in the parking lot of a church on Lincoln Road. Maybe he hoped the animal got killed, he wasn't sure himself, what he was attempting to accomplish. However, Paradise Animal Shelter was nearby, so perhaps someone from there would notice the dog wandering around and pick him up.

What Bryant did was, at the very least, good for a laugh because he was willing to bet his ex-wife, Marsha, assumed the dog got out of the backyard by itself. She happened to be prettier than she was intelligent. The problem was his girlfriend was exactly the same thing, just a younger version. Even though Bryant returned a couple house keys when he left, who said he might not have yet another key? Marsha was too dumb to think of that, let alone change the locks. Instead she wasted money on some heavy-duty padlocks for the two gates leading to the backyard.

If what Bryant did messed up his daughter, Mona, too bad. Her mother was way too protective of her, and the sooner Mona got a taste of what life was really like, the better.

MORE DOGS AND THEIR TWISTED TALES–
AND ONE CAT STORY

See? Bryant was the better parent. What got him the most pissed was he couldn't let Mona meet his girlfriend, Pam—or anyone else he was with, unless he was married to the woman. Supposedly that was decided by "The Court," but Marsha had to be behind the ruling all the way.

Pam's standing as Bryant's girlfriend wasn't a forever thing by any means, he was willing to allow. Right now he had no place of his own, so living at her cushy apartment was A-O.K. with him. Although the apartment complex allowed dogs (under seventy pounds), Pam didn't have a dog, which was fine with Bryant, although he didn't dare say as much. Until he could put enough money together to buy his own place (at this point one mortgage was enough), he planned on staying put and would be on his best behavior— as long as things remained as they were and Pam didn't decide they had to marry, have a kid or get a dog.

A potential problem could occur with the dog-owning status of Pam because she'd had dogs in her family when growing up, and her mother in particular was "dog crazy" (Pam's description). If nothing else, Pam might be called upon to dog sit for her mother at some point. Supposedly her mother currently didn't have a dog either, and hopefully that didn't change. All Bryant asked was to have his own place before Pam decided to bring a mutt home.

Pam had gotten to the point she wanted Bryant and her mother to meet. He had suggested meeting for lunch one day during the week, but Pam had nixed that, saying, "My mom will be the only one not dressed well enough to even go in a fast-food place. Well, she'd look O.K. probably, but she might not smell the greatest."

With that kind of intro to Mrs. Rhonda Martenowsky's life, how could Bryant possibly appear rude by proceeding to ask what she did for a living? He'd simply ask her when they met face-to-face, which was hopefully a sure thing at some point. As it was, there had yet to be a mention of Dad, other than a remark that included "poor Dad." Given the tone of

111

Pam's voice when it was uttered, Dad was no longer. Even though her job as a paralegal at "Shreiner, Merle, and Dobson" probably paid pretty well, it was possible she was the beneficiary of a generous life insurance policy.

Early afternoon at "Sunrise Insurance," where Bryant worked in the claims department (coincidentally enough), he got a call from none other than Pam. He HATED when she used the company phone to get ahold of him. He was certain she did it just to call the office and ask the secretary, Cindy, if he was available. It wasn't like Cindy was exclusively for him. Besides, Pam knew his cell phone number and used that 99.9% of the time, whether calling or texting him. If there was an inside joke behind calling Sunrise Insurance directly, Bryant missed it.

Pam was all chatty with Bryant, irritating him to the point he was almost compelled to remind her she was at work, too. Then she sprang this on him: "I wanted to warn you, we're going to have an overnight guest tonight."

"Oh?" Bryant said, trying to sound like he was ready for anything.

"Yes," Pam replied. "My mom just called to say she took a dog for someone as a personal favor. An older lady had to give him up for whatever reason. Mom just realized tonight happens to be 'casino night' and she stays out until three a.m. for this monthly event. This outing is really going to be a blow-out because one of her friends is turning seventy, so the four of them might be out all night. Long story short, since my mom just took this dog in, she wants me to take care of him overnight."

"Uh...O.K.," Bryant said, mostly confused. He knew he ought to feel something else too, but he couldn't seem to get to that place. Maybe he was relieved "the dog" wasn't yet a permanent fixture. He wanted to tell Pam, "Could you at least cook something good for dinner?" However, he didn't want to start ordering her around, although he helped out with her rent and expenses, which was in addition to all the financial obligations he had to his "former" family. Sometimes Bryant wished he hadn't taken them for granted, the dog included.

Just after three o'clock, Bryant got a call on his cell phone from his ex-wife, Marsha. She'd just picked up Mona at school, and she (Mona) had a horrible toothache. The dentist's office had already been contacted, and Bryant would have to take her to Dr. Danner's as soon as possible after he left work.

"Is she really in a lot of pain?" Bryant asked.

Rather than answer his question, Marsha told Bryant, "I'm sorry if you had plans for after work or whatever."

"I'm not trying to get out of taking Mona to the dentist, Marsha."

"Well, I wouldn't have made the appointment if I thought she was faking how much pain she's in."

"Fine." Bryant said. "That's all I need to hear. I should be able to sneak out of here by four, unless something comes up."

"I'll see you shortly then," Marsha said and hung up.

One thing about being on "speaking terms" with your ex-wife: it didn't come with a guarantee she would be friendly. Anyway, Bryant had to call Pam and tell her he probably wouldn't be home as soon as expected. Then again, she had her "overnight guest" to keep her company, so she might not even notice he was late.

After some thought, Bryant decided the best way to contact Pam was via a text: "I have to take my daughter to the dentist after I get out of here. Hoped to be home by 5 but will be late."

Immediately Pam shot back this text: "Why can't Marsha take her? My surprise is effed. I wuz looking forward to a super-long evening together."

Bryant texted back: "SORRY!!!! Marsha knows who has to pay the bill."

Pam replied with this text: "I get it. I'll be waiting."

Approaching the house (where Marsha and Mona lived),

Bryant felt so badly he could hardly pull into the driveway and make it known he was at "the scene of the crime."

Fortunately Bryant didn't even have to exit his vehicle because Mona came running out the front door as if being pursued by a monster. Her "eagerness" to go to the dentist was due to something besides how much pain she was in. Bryant wasn't about to accuse Marsha of being a terrible mother because he sure as hell didn't want to take care of his own kid! As it was, the judge presiding over their divorce about fell over himself trying to accommodate Marsha. The guy didn't even hint she ought to at least get a part-time job. Meanwhile, Bryant was expected to allow Marsha to maintain her current lifestyle. Cad though he was, couldn't he catch a break?

Bryant had somehow fallen in love with Marsha, but nowadays he felt the exact opposite toward her. She was obsessed with exercise to the point she appeared insane. Maybe if she toned it down a little, but her ass was suddenly firmer....

Driving to Dr. Danner's, Bryant might as well have been alone in the car because Mona didn't say a word. Bryant almost started to make conversation, but he kept wanting to say, "Too bad about Bugsby, kiddo." Since he had enough compassion to not mention the dog, silence prevailed the duration of the trip.

It was never easy to sit in a waiting room, but on this occasion it was a breeze. Pam kept sending Bryant extremely seductive texts. Before he knew it, Mona reappeared and it was time to pay the bill. Never before did he write a check while smiling.

Bryant didn't have to see Marsha when he had picked up Mona, nor did he have to see her when he dropped her off. However, "someone" opened the side door for Mona. Once it was closed, Bryant believed his daughter was in safe hands. Despite Bryant's criticisms of Marsha, he was willing to allow she was a decent mother. As mentioned, Bryant wanted no part of raising their daughter. Paying for everything was more than enough responsibility. If Marsha wanted to ignore him, it was still preferable to having her scream at him "for no reason at all."

Suddenly Bryant recalled the sexy texts of Pam's. He'd signed off with: "On my way home!"

Pam texted back: "SEE U SOON I'M ... ready! Hope you're hungry cuz I slaved in the kitchen. LOL!"

Fortunately Pam's place wasn't far; Bryant was starving, among other things.

Minimal though the distance was, Bryant was impatient to get there—but not to fill his stomach. His mind was still on Pam's racy texts, and he hoped she was as horny as she'd previously revealed. Dinner could wait.

Upon Bryant's arrival at Pam's apartment, he remembered to knock once and wait a few seconds before unlocking the door (as instructed in a text). When he opened it, Pam was standing on the other side, wearing a short, sheer white silk negligee and nothing underneath. Studying his expression, she smiled slyly.

Bryant wanted to take her in his arms and carry her to the bedroom. For the time being he was satisfied with having a make-out session with her in the entryway. However, he wasn't too distracted to fail to hear the clicking of a dog's nails on the white tile floor in the kitchen, which was on the other side of a wall. That was the dog Pam had mentioned taking care of overnight for her mother. At least it wasn't someone's kid, or they'd have to heed some decorum and stop making out.

Nonetheless, Bryant immediately did upon seeing "the dog" was none other than Bugsby! This was altogether too coincidental, but maybe it was what he deserved. What completely unnerved Bryant was having the dog make eye contact with him, despite the fact Bryant was so embarrassed he wanted to look away! It was even possible Bugsby briefly stuck his tongue out at Bryant, but the dog was probably licking his lips.

Pam finally piped up: "Oh there's Beethoven. He's the dog my mom took in for a retired music teacher-lady who had to give him up but didn't want him just thrown in a cage until he was adopted."

"Do you believe everything your mother tells you?" Bryant asked, although he didn't really care what Pam's answer would be because he had enough other problems at this point.

"Yeah, I do," Pam said. "Besides, why would she lie about a dog? She's the director at Paradise Animal Shelter. She sees dogs and cats come and go all day."

Bryant didn't say anything else because there were two guilty parties and he was one of them. He was too devastated to clear up the whole mess, which was what needed to be done.

On a whim, Marsha took a different route for her jog, the morning after Bugsby "disappeared." She still ran along the canal but went east toward Scottsdale Road, versus west, toward 56th Street. In seemingly no time at all she reached Scottsdale Road and wanted to jog another block, but she was too impatient to wait for all the traffic to pass. As it was, Mona had mentioned she needed to be at school a few minutes earlier than usual, not saying why.

Rather than at least jog on the other (south) side of the canal for the return trip, Marsha opted to simply turn around. Upon doing so she noticed a man's body was floating face down in the water, wearing an orange T-shirt and black shorts. Bryant occasionally power-walked, and his favorite outfit was an orange T-shirt he received from Mona for Father's Day that read "World's Greatest Dad!" on the front. (Marsha and he were still married when he got that gift.) The body looked like it was a match for Bryant's, and the thick, dark brown hair on the corpse's head, appeared to confirm as much. Still, Marsha needed one more clue.

MORE DOGS AND THEIR TWISTED TALES–
AND ONE CAT STORY

It was impossible to "just keep running," even if Marsha was mistaken about the identity of the dead body. Fortunately she always had her phone with her, so she called 9-1-1. After identifying herself and her location, she told the dispatcher what she saw and then added, "I think the man might be my ex-husband," before bursting into tears.

The dispatcher briefly consoled Marsha, but it wasn't helpful. The last thing Marsha wanted to do was wait for the emergency personnel to arrive, so she started jogging back toward home. As it was, how much longer would it be "home" for Mona and herself, given the circumstances? With that thought, Marsha ran the rest of the way home.

As Marsha approached "her" house, she could see a gray hatchback parked in the driveway. She wasn't yet close enough to see the make or model of the car, but it unnerved her to see anyone parked there, with Mona alone in the house. She didn't even have Bugsby to keep her company. It shouldn't have been a crime to leave the dog in the backyard for thirty minutes!

Marsha was out of breath because of running so hard, but her nervousness combined with her protectiveness made her ready to defend "her" property.

The second Marsha reached the opened driver's side window of what turned out to be a Honda with darkly-tinted windows, she knew exactly who she was looking at: Bryant's girlfriend, Pam Martenowsky. Marsha knew her name and her face but never knew what she drove. Not feeling exactly hospitable, Marsha asked, "What do you want?"

Pam replied, "Bryant was acting strange before going for a fifteen-minute walk along the canal. He never came home, so I decided to stop here on the way to my mom's, thinking maybe he was here with you. He has to make a clean break from you or forget it."

"No, hon, he's not here, never was, never will be, at least I don't think," Marsha said, her voice dripping with sarcasm. She was about to go in the house when she heard a dog whimper from inside Pam's vehicle. That caused Marsha to ask Pam, "Do you have a dog in your car?"

"Yes, I do," Pam replied.

"Could I see him for a sec?" Marsha asked, suddenly less harsh-sounding.

Pam shrugged and lowered the window of the passenger window behind her. Immediately none other than Bugsby stuck his head out, causing Marsha to exclaim, "Bugsy! I can't believe it!"

In turn, Pam shut the window again, almost catching Bugsby's nose. Since she was apparently oblivious to as much, Marsha pointed it out, saying, "You almost caught Bugsby's nose in the window just now. By the way, he's my family's dog, and someone must have stolen him from the backyard. Was it you?"

"No," Pam answered. Then she started her car and began backing up, only to be stopped by Marsha, who reached in the window and grabbed the steering wheel. Rather than start a physical and/or verbal fight, Pam stopped the vehicle. She only did so because she didn't want any trouble with her boyfriend's ex-wife.

Not only that, Pam decided to be really generous and let the dog out, so Mrs. Morrow could take him in the house. The dog couldn't wait to get out of the vehicle. Not only was he cramped in there, but he did indeed appear to know who his "real owner" was. He also knew exactly where "home" was, and Mrs. Morrow had to hang on tightly to his leash as he headed straight for the front door of the house.

Watching the two of them, Pam muttered, "Mom's full of shit, just as I should have suspected."

She Becomes Her

The key to harmony between Cal (Calvin) and Jo (Joely) Greff was Cal always cut his wife plenty of slack. And that was to say he was understanding, sympathetic, open-minded, etc. He was a computer nerd, not a "creative type" like she was. Also, she had OCD (obsessive-compulsive disorder).

Unfortunately (?) Cal and Jo's son inherited a "lazy gene," but it wasn't from either one of them. He managed to graduate from high school but just barely. Then he spent the summer being a bum.

What lit a fire under Brad was he realized Mom loved having him lay around because she was mortified there would be an empty nest if he left. Also, she feared not being of any use to him anymore. Cal's company was obviously taken for granted, which Cal initially found funny.

Once Brad "flew the coop" he first attended Barnett Bicycle Institute in Colorado Springs, Colorado, for a two-week bicycle repair course. Afterward he was on his way to college at the University of Colorado at Boulder. With his new-found knowledge he got a job at a Boulder bike shop, enabling him to support himself while going to school (although his parents helped pay for the first year's tuition). There was hope for him yet.

Meanwhile, with Brad having left the nest, Jo proceeded to plunge full-force into her artistic world, creating dozens of paper cut-out pictures that sold for hundreds of dollars apiece—and she couldn't keep up with the demand! Cal was happy for her—and for them as a couple, why not? The rate

Amy Kristoff

they were going, they could pay off their mortgage early, relieving both of them of a burden.

Best of all, Jo was staying busy, which was important in her case. As "simple" as her cut-out pictures were, Cal was aware she spent a lot of time just designing them. Thus far the majority of Jo's pictures had themes geared toward young children (jungle scenes with comical-looking monkeys and plenty of vines and colorful flowers were popular). It was possible Jo would start experimenting with more "adult" themes for her cut-outs. There would be no limit to what she could create, once she became more and more confident. Would potential fortune and fame go to Jo's head? Cal wasn't being silly; with his wife's OCD, what he feared was her becoming so immersed in her artwork she'd literally work herself to death.

Living in a gated condominium community in Scottsdale, Arizona, the Greffs didn't have to bother with yardwork because it was included in the monthly association fee. When Cal returned from work in the evening, he didn't have to do anything more than make a vodka tonic and sit down to watch cable news until Jo announced dinner was ready. Ever since her artwork became so popular, occasionally there was a wait until the meal was on the table. However, Cal didn't mind getting slightly inebriated while waiting. Ever since Brad finally left, Cal had admittedly let his guard down a bit. Meanwhile, Jo didn't drink before and still didn't. Anymore she was so immersed in her artwork, she didn't have time to unwind, instead going straight from working nonstop to falling into bed, exhausted.

On this particular early November evening, Cal parked his Nissan Murano under the carport, thinking it would be a quiet, relaxing evening at home. Instead, the second he opened the front door, Jo could be heard crying in the back of the condo, where Cal had converted a spare (third) bedroom into Jo's workplace.

Cal found Jo sitting cross-legged on the white tile floor,

120

her face red, eyes puffy. Upon seeing Cal she declared, "Mom's dead." Then she burst into tears again.

This sounded insensitive, but Cal wanted to say, "Jo, honey, your mom did you a favor by finally expiring. It seemed like more and more, all she did was call you every day to complain about something." Instead Cal got down on the floor with Jo and put his arms around her, saying, "I'm so sorry! Why didn't you call me at work or my cell phone?"

"I just got the word," Jo replied. "I'd taken her to the hospital for some tests because she wasn't feeling well. Nothing had been found wrong with her so far, but she was spending the night for observation. I was going to see her after dinner, before visiting hours ended. I was trying to get caught up on my picture orders. Then I get this call that she's already gone!"

Jo burst into loud sobs after talking, and Cal held her close, hoping to console her. Undoubtedly she felt guilty for doing her own fair share of complaining, namely about her mother! Then this thought came to Cal: What about Constance's (Jo's mother) dog?

Cal asked Jo about Kitty (a Keeshond), and she immediately sat up straight and admitted, "I totally forgot about her, poor girl. I let her out in Mom's yard that's not much bigger than ours, before we went to the hospital, but I haven't been back there. I guess all this has been too much for me to take." Then she started sobbing again.

"I'll go get Kitty, for starters," Cal said, as he was knowledgeable about dogs, having grown up in a family that always had one (and he was inevitably the one expected to walk "the dog," which quickly went from a chore to something he looked forward to).

Cal started to get up, but first he had to console Jo some more. The two embraced for a few seconds before Cal was on his way, leaving Jo to finish her latest cut-out picture. She promised dinner would be on the table upon Cal's return with Constance's dog.

It had been tempting to ask Jo if she had everything covered regarding her mother and making burial arrangements, but Cal was glad he didn't say anything. There would be a time to ask her when he returned with her mother's dog. Hopefully dinner would actually be served, and they would have a new subject about which to make conversation. Cal liked to sneak table scraps to a dog, which was a huge no-no at home, growing up. Finally Cal could have some fun, giving a dog a treat, and he was pretty sure his mother-in-law spoiled Kitty with tidbits of food, so the dog would be expecting something while Cal and Jo were eating.

Although Kitty was initially wary of Cal when he showed up at his mother-in-law's, the dog quickly warmed to him and was eager to leave with him, particularly after he said, "Let's go for a car ride, Kitty."

The only problem was after Cal had driven away from the house with the dog in the back of his silver Murano did he realize all he had besides the dog was a leash. So back to the house he went, grabbing a couple bowls and Kitty's food, as well as the dog's bed and some supplies.

Finally Cal and Kitty were on their way home. Jo had better have dinner on the table for sure by this time. However, with Jo's mother's passing, he was willing to give her some leeway—for the time being. It needed to be pointed out Jo overall had a "difficult" relationship with her mother, and Jo admitted she once actually told her, "Sometimes I wish you would die!"

Of course Jo was quick to clarify she stated the aforementioned during adolescence, so what she'd said "didn't really count." Nonetheless, Cal always kept that remark in the back of his head. What also stayed with him was the (supposed) retort of Jo's mother: "Careful what you wish for, Joely."

Once home, Kitty was quick to reconnect with Joely, since they knew one another. Admittedly Cal did not know the dog because he rarely went to his mother-in-law's. (And no, Cal didn't know his mother-in-law, Constance, very well, either.) It wasn't as if they didn't get along; Constance liked to keep to herself, and Cal never spent any more time with her than Jo made him. It wasn't an indictment on Cal's mother-in-law; Cal wasn't even close to his own family. Not only that, they all lived halfway across the country, and the last time he saw any of them was a few years ago, shortly before both his parents passed away within a few months of one another. There wasn't a funeral for either one because his sister, Claire, was against it. There was no arguing with Claire; describing her as highly-opinionated was an understatement. Cal had long ago resigned himself to loving his older sister without actually liking her. In the meantime he'd continue to keep his distance. She had her (second) husband and three stepkids to keep her busy, so he rarely heard from her.

Sometimes Cal felt like a dog because he lived for dinner; it was the most important meal (versus breakfast). Therefore, he was especially "happy" to see dinner was on the table in the kitchen, where Jo and Cal usually ate. Jo was nowhere to be seen, but her yellow Mazda Miata was under the two-vehicle carport. She probably went back in her workshop to finish some more pictures.

Sure enough, Kitty found Jo, as Cal heard their exchange of greetings, particularly Jo, talking like a little kid to the dog (or talking to the dog like she was a kid?). It was soothing to hear her sound happy and carefree, as he was aware she was grieving.

Cal let the two enjoy each other's company in the other room while he sat down to eat. He was starving! He proceeded to serve himself a liberal helping of the chicken noodle casserole in a dish in the middle of the table. After he ate a couple bites, Jo appeared, Kitty right on her heels. Neither one looked like she had a care in the world. Truthfully? They both seemed kind of weird all of a sudden. Cal decided to concentrate on eating. It'd been a long day.

The second Jo sat down to Cal's right, Kitty sat between them but stared expectantly at Jo, ignoring Cal. He remarked, "She must be waiting for a treat or two."

"No, Kitty's not getting anything from me," Jo said. "Mom probably gave her something, but that seems messy and completely gross."

"Are you kidding?" Cal exclaimed. "There's no harm in me giving Kitty a tiny piece of chicken. The dog hasn't eaten all day."

Jo started to get up, declaring, "I'll feed her then, using her food."

"Jo, please, sit down," Cal told her. "Kitty's fine for now. She's probably pretty stressed right now, but luckily she knows you."

"O.K., whatever, dog expert."

Since Jo still hadn't eaten anything, Kitty changed her focus to Cal, who was shoveling casserole into his mouth like there was no tomorrow. However, he managed to stop eating long enough to discreetly give Kitty a tiny sliver of chicken. She carefully took it as if she were a pro. She didn't even touch any of Cal's fingers with her mouth or tongue, so he didn't have to leap up and wash his hands. He wanted to say, "Good girl," but he feared Jo would get upset.

Nonetheless, Jo was sitting right there so of course she saw everything (and she had yet to eat anything). "How could you do that?" she asked, shaking her head. "You'd better wash your hand because I'm not going to keep sitting here unless you do."

Cal wanted to tell his wife to simply pretend she didn't see what she just did. Then he reminded himself she was grieving and needed to be humored at a time like this. He obediently got up to wash his hand(s).

Upon Cal's return to the table, he was relieved to see Jo had a serving of casserole on her plate. However, she looked ready to cry. Kitty was laying down, not asleep but certainly not expecting a treat from Jo. Cal almost started crying too.

What was up? To describe himself as stoical wasn't exactly a stretch and he was proud of as much. It should have made it easy to ask Jo if she'd made burial/funeral arrangements for her mother. However, right now it was too much of a test for everyone to do so, so he'd have to wait until morning. If nothing else, surely a representative from the hospital would contact Jo and get the necessary information.

Rather than cry, Jo proceeded to start babbling about the recipients of the two completed cut-out pictures: a six-year-old boy, Curtis, and his mother, Theresa. They'd recently moved to Scottsdale from San Diego, where "Dad" still lived. Jo stated, "No one said a word about divorce, so it sounds like they're living apart for the time being. Theresa paid in full in cash before I even started the pictures. I only request fifty-percent, so I felt like I needed to at least finish them on time. I'm even going to hang them for Theresa because she asked me to. I am so flattered."

"Good, honey," Cal told his wife. Then he heaped on more praise by adding, "I always believed in your artistic talent. It's great you can reap some financial benefit too." Then he couldn't wait to shovel some more casserole into his mouth.

Jo must have finally taken Cal's cue, and she too was eating but not with nearly as much enthusiasm.

It was hardly surprising Kitty was watching Cal with much more interest than she was watching Jo. Therefore, Cal found it impossible not to give Kitty another small piece of chicken. He defied Jo to protest.

Jo didn't but that made Cal feel worse. Although he did not feel Kitty touch his fingers at all, he felt obligated to get up and wash his hand again. Anyway he was suddenly full, so he left the table and took his empty plate with him.

Bedtime couldn't come soon enough for Cal, All the stress Jo was feeling after losing her mother was rubbing off on Cal, something like that. The bottom line was he was exhausted and couldn't wait for the day to end.

As a matter of fact Jo had taken a shower and "went to bed" shortly after cleaning up the dinner dishes. She said she was going to do some reading, which was not unusual for her. Even though they had a super TV in their bedroom, she preferred not to watch it. Cal was the one who liked to watch it until he became drowsy enough to fall asleep. He never failed to hit the power button on the remote control before actually falling asleep. Otherwise Jo would have a fit—the next morning. Why didn't Jo turn off the TV herself? Her excuse: "I don't know how to use the remote." Even worse: she claimed to be "afraid" to touch the buttons on the TV itself.

Earlier, Cal had managed to ask Jo if she had been in contact with the hospital regarding final arrangements for her mother. Jo nodded her response. Cal had decided that would suffice as a reply for the time being. Again, he didn't want to push Jo, knowing how mentally fragile she was.

Cal wasn't taking another shower until tomorrow morning before work, so he slipped into his pajamas and laid in bed too, without Jo even looking at him. Only once the covers were over him and his eyes were already closed (the TV wasn't on) did Jo finally deign to acknowledge him, saying, "Kitty needs to go on one last, short walk. That's what Mom would do with her before they went to bed. Where is Kitty now?"

"In her bed, at the foot of our bed," Cal replied and tried to close his eyes but he was too tense to keep laying down. He proceeded to throw back the covers on his side of the king-sized bed and declared, "I'll take Kitty out right now." It was impossible to relax at this point anyway, until appeasing his wife. He did, however, mumble, "I let her out in the yard for a couple minutes. She did her business and was ready to come in."

As Cal was changing from his pajama bottoms to a pair of jeans, Jo asked him, "Did you bring the poop bags from Mom's?"

MORE DOGS AND THEIR TWISTED TALES–
AND ONE CAT STORY

"Yes I did," Cal replied. (He only did so because when he'd made his return trip to get Kitty's food, bowls, and bed, a whole roll of purple waste bags were in plain sight.) If he wasn't familiar with dogs he would have ignored the bags.

Fortunately once Kitty saw the leash she got right up and was eager to go outside. Thankfully Cal had that much going for him regarding this unplanned walk. The last thing he would have wanted to do was drag Kitty outside. That would have compelled Cal to go right back to bed, and the evening would have ended in divorce. Seriously, Cal did not trust Jo at a time like this, to react instantaneously to her emotions and do something she'd (hopefully) later regret.

As obliging as Kitty was to go on a short walk, she had no interest in relieving herself, not even urinating again. Obviously she was finished for the night (and Cal was in agreement). So they went home and both went straight to their respective beds. Jo was still reading and Cal told her, "Just as I figured, she didn't need to go anymore."

Jo managed to stop reading long enough to arch an eyebrow and that was it. Cal immediately became defensive but didn't dare say a word.

The next morning Cal didn't need the alarm clock to wake him at seven a.m. because at that time Jo was screaming, "Kitty left a huge pile of shit right by the nightstand, not two inches from my new satin slippers! Ugh!"

Given the fact almost the whole house had Saltillo-tiled floor, it wasn't like the crap would be difficult to clean up. Cal got right up and made sure to let Kitty out, who was sitting by the closed bedroom door. At least she knew "outside" was where she was supposed to relieve herself.

"She's probably stressed about losing her owner," Cal said, to which Jo muttered, "I doubt that has anything to do with what she did. If she's smart enough to be stressed out, she shit there because she can't stand me. Or maybe she thinks I did something to my mother."

Cal just nodded and took Kitty out. While she was in the

127

walled courtyard, Cal went back in the house and grabbed a whole roll of paper towels to clean up the mess.

Jo was still in bed, apparently having fallen back to sleep. Cal took care of the mess and went to the carport to throw-away the soiled paper towels. Fortunately Jo only bought deodorized garbage bags.

"You hungry, Kitty?" Cal asked the dog as he stood out-side the six-foot tall, black wrought-iron gate leading to the walled courtyard. Unless someone opened the gate and let Kitty out, she couldn't escape. If she did, would she try to go "home"? She appeared to accept the situation, but maybe that was only because Jo was familiar to her.

Why did he even wonder about any of this? Cal asked himself. He was going to be late for work at this rate. He'd have to start getting up earlier so he could take Kitty for a walk before he had to leave for the day. It'd sure help if Jo would take even a small interest in Kitty, so she could walk her in the morning. Given her creative streak she needed to look at an activity like that as an opportunity for inspiration.

With Kitty fed, Cal went back in the bedroom, where Jo was not only still sleeping, she appeared to be in a coma. And he wasn't trying to be funny. He'd unfailingly been a "Yes, Dear" kind of husband, so something in him must have final-ly snapped because he stood right over his wife and demand-ed to know, "Are you getting up? It's almost seven-thirty."

Jo's eyes popped open and she looked furious, which Cal took to mean he just pissed her off, no surprise. She liked to wake up "on her own terms." Rather than scream at him, however, she sat up and declared, "I honestly do not know what happened. I was going to get up after I went out of my mind about Kitty's poop. I don't know what got into me. It's not like I didn't change my fair share of Brad's diapers."

Cal nodded. That was the most reasonable remark he'd ever heard from his wife. She wasn't one who was good at putting things in perspective. She'd overslept and could sud-denly put things in perspective? It was possible her mother's death had forced some perspective on her, but Jo would need more than that to "get it." For her to change, something supernatural would have to occur. Cal suddenly felt anxious, considering as much. Maybe he too was really upset about his mother-in-law's passing.

His shower taken, Cal quickly dressed and then went to the back door to bring Kitty inside. She was sitting in the far corner of the courtyard, looking forlorn. He called her and she immediately came to him. He told her he might take her for a walk when he got home but would definitely do so tomorrow morning, hopefully starting a daily ritual.

Cal then turned around and there was Jo, looking very annoyed. She also looked strange, yet he couldn't figure out what was different about her, which bothered him.

Luckily Cal wasn't hungry for breakfast because Jo hadn't even begun to make anything. Nothing was elaborate with Jo, but she usually managed to at least toast a couple pieces of bread and slather margarine on them, which was plenty to eat. She almost constantly had coffee brewing, so at least Cal could have a cup before leaving for the day. As it was, he felt worse about not taking Kitty for a walk than for missing breakfast. Cal could indulge more at dinner tonight—and give Kitty an extra treat or two, Jo be damned. (He was just kidding!)

Cal let Kitty in the house with Jo still staring, her eyes like daggers. He pretended not to notice and calmly asked her, "Will you be O.K. with Kitty for the day, or should I come home on my lunch break and check on you two?"

"We'll be fine, Cal," Jo replied. "I've never 'taken care of Kitty' as far as daily care, but I've fed her and let her out, usually when my mom's around."

Something was definitely going on. It wasn't a bad thing by any means, but Cal's sense of unease refused to lessen. At the same time, he wasn't worried about Kitty; he had a feeling Jo would take good care of her.

Jo was never so happy to have the day to herself—minus

her husband or anyone else, save her mother's dog, Kitty. Jo was supposed to go to the hospital to sign some papers she didn't take care of the day before. First she'd finish a couple more pictures and then head that way. Also, she might take Kitty for a walk, something the two of them had never done together.

Truthfully, Jo used to think naming a dog "Kitty" was completely stupid, but she'd changed her mind. Jo's mother obviously thought the name fit, and Jo had to agree.

Kitty had been following Jo around the house, but it didn't bother Jo at all. Even though she wasn't into dogs, it was evident she very much enjoyed having a dog for company. Thankfully Kitty wasn't staring at her strangely, or Jo might have become paranoid. Admittedly she could be kind of ridiculous like that.

Joely's brother, Reg (Reginald), had been estranged from their mother for a number of years. (He'd lost count, it had been so long.) However, he still resided in the Phoenix area, where he had a successful dental practice. He wasn't even aware their mother passed away until Jo called him at his dentistry office. He stayed late most evenings, so she knew to contact him there. Reg was one of the few remaining individuals who still preferred to talk on a land line, above all else (and he detested e-mailing, texting and cell phones in general). Call him "behind the times," but he cleared a quarter of a million a year after expenses, so he was doing something right with his life. He couldn't keep his marriage intact, but that was his ex-wife's fault because she was the cheating one.

How Reg's and Jo's mother, Constance, treated her husband when he was ailing was what caused the rift between Reg and her. With Constance gone, Reg wanted to tell Jo about as much, but he wasn't sure if she would even believe him. She always thought the world of their mother, but Reg felt the need to "clear his name," if only in his mind.

MORE DOGS AND THEIR TWISTED TALES–
AND ONE CAT STORY

Currently Reg was renting a house in Cave Creek, not far from his dental practice. He wanted to live closer to where his old house was, in Scottsdale, but there was nothing available for lease that was to his liking. With what he made he could "afford" to be particular. He wanted to buy a house at some point, but he was still mentally hurting from having given his ex-wife his beloved house as part of the divorce settlement. Their twin boys were already grown and gone, so she couldn't wait to move her boyfriend into the spacious house. The guy didn't even have a regular job, and he was in for a surprise if he thought Fran (Francine) was going to take care of him forever. Rumor had it she was already cheating on the guy. Once she ran out of money, he'd leave anyway.

As for Reg's sister, Jo, she appeared to have made a good choice for a husband in Cal Greff. He was a computer nerd, but other than that, he seemed to be a straight-up kind of guy. Although Reg moved in entirely different social circles from his sister and her husband, he would have been happy to spend more time with them than he did.

Morning was the best time to get ahold of Jo. As the day progressed, both she and Reg seemed to get too busy to answer each one's respective phone calls.

So Reg called his sister, expecting her to answer and she did—but she sounded different, almost exactly like her mother. There was no forgetting his mother's voice, despite how long it had been since the two had conversed.

The similarity of Jo's voice to their mother's was so eerie, Reg hesitated to exchange greetings with her. It turned out he was more affected by their mother's death than might have been assumed. All Reg wanted was to explain himself to his sister, as he wanted it made clear there was a valid reason behind his behavior.

Jo proceeded to mention her husband, Cal, saved the day by thinking of Mom's dog, Kitty, left alone in her house. She confessed to being "too overwhelmed with grief to think straight."

Reg told her, "Jo, that's completely understandable. I'm sorry I haven't been more accessible in regard to Mom, but I like to think I have a sound argument as to why I basically cut her out of my life."

"To be honest, Reg? I'm not in any condition to listen to what you might want to tell me, not right now."

"I just wanted to get it off my chest," Reg admitted.

"That's understandable, but I kind of have an idea what it might be about."

"You do?"

"Yes."

"How?"

"Let's just saying by using some...logic."

"Oh. O.K.," Reg said but he was utterly confused. Was it possible Jo had a secret she needed to share too? He started to say more, but Jo abruptly said good-bye and hung up, just like that, which was totally unlike her. Now that Mom was dead obviously Jo was super-pissed at him, and he didn't blame her. It was more important than ever he clarify himself. His sister had always meant so much to him, and the last thing Reg wanted was to have her lose respect for him.

Jo was surprised her brother Reg just called. It appeared he wanted to explain why he had cut Mom out of his life. Mom never said a word about why, so it had been safe to assume it had to do with how Mom treated Dad when he became very ill with terminal cancer. She never would have admitted to abusing him but did confess to "feeling resentful" toward him as he became more sick. He'd refused any chemo treatments because he was told it would do more harm than good in his case. (He would die even sooner.) Reg obviously saw something one day without Mom having any idea her son was a witness. That wouldn't have been a surprise, as Reg visited their father every morning for an hour, the last couple months George was alive. The two had been very close in Reg's youth, and Dad had been extremely proud of his

son's accomplishments. Although their father provided well
for his family, he considered himself a "tradesman" who
never went to college but managed to make something of
himself. The respect he had for Reg was boundless. Reg
could but return the respect at the end of his father's life. Jo
was relieved Reg took that task upon himself because Jo was
never close to their father at any point of her life. She saw
very little of him because he worked so much and in turn had
minimal interaction with him.

Constance was relieved when her husband had a fatal
heart attack one morning when she was attempting to give
him a sponge bath. She felt guilty about her relief, confessing
as much to Jo without any hesitation. She even added, "I
couldn't believe how heavy his body suddenly became when
he had no control over it anymore. And here I'd thought he
was a pain in the neck to hold up before."

Mom couldn't wait to give away almost all of Dad's things.
Initially Jo had been alarmed by her mother's actions.
Looking back, what her mother did was probably driven by
guilt, and she wanted to be "done" with every element of her
husband, despite her love and devotion to him.

Jo was awakened from her reverie by another phone call,
this time from Theresa Fuller, the woman whose pictures
were finished the night before and who wanted Jo to hang
them when they were ready.

The women exchanged pleasantries, and Theresa asked
Jo when she'd be available to hang the pictures, provided
they were finished.

"They're done," Jo told Theresa. "I can hang them today
if you want."

"Wonderful."

"I skipped going back to the hospital to take care of something after my mother died, just so I could stay home and finish the pictures for you and your son, Curtis."

"I'm so sorry to hear about your loss," Theresa said.

"Thank you. I'm dealing with the situation the best I can."

Jo was floored by her admission concerning losing her mother. Usually she was very private about her personal life. It wasn't like she wanted any sympathy. She'd already gotten plenty from complete strangers.

"I'm free the rest of this morning, so maybe you can come over now?"

"Didn't you mention your house is only a couple miles from mine?"

"Yes," Theresa replied. "The address is five-two-eight Palmdale Way."

"I have to go back to the hospital and then I'll be over your way. It shouldn't be more than an hour."

"Great. See you then."

After the good-byes, it occurred to Jo she had Kitty to contend with before making her departure. She considered calling Cal at work, asking him if he could come home for lunch after all and take care of Kitty (let her out and feed her). Then she actually thought about what taking care of the dog entailed and realized she could do it herself. In fact, she let Kitty out and fed her from time to time at her mother's but never on a daily basis. It was time to add something to her schedule, was all. She looked forward to being needed again. Ever since her son left home, she'd felt useless. She just hoped Kitty didn't leave any more piles of poop by the bed. If Jo also took her on walks, maybe they could form a bond. Despite Cal telling Kitty he would walk her, Jo just might have to "steal" that activity from him. Either that or Kitty was about to become a very exhausted dog.

"That looks perfect," Theresa told Jo, the latter having hung the fourth and final picture that had been delivered to Ms. Fuller's home. This was the easiest and most rewarding part of Jo's day thus far. Having gone to the hospital prior to this stop, Jo immediately felt depressed about losing her mother, not that a feeling of sadness wasn't already following her around. However, she refused to let herself be in a funk and would continue to stay as busy as possible. Meanwhile, her mother never seemed to have enough to do, which Jo maintained was unhealthy for her, especially after losing her husband. At least she'd liked dogs, or she might not have lived a decade and a half longer than her husband.

It was imperative Jo like dogs too, simple as that. Although she didn't expect to outlive Cal, it was possible she would. One thing she didn't want to do was look for another husband. She was fine by herself, provided she had some sort of companionship. She wasn't planning on seeing much of their son, Brad. At college in Colorado, he was so enamored with the "awesome" climate, he never wanted to come back to the Phoenix area. Cal was thrilled with their son's attitude because it had formerly looked as if he'd never leave the house at all, let alone permanently move out of the state. He'd even vowed to pay his own tuition next year, working as many jobs as necessary to do so. So he wasn't lazy, after all.

Jo was on her way home and she couldn't wait to see Kitty. She needed someone to hug all of a sudden, and a dog would do. It came down to wanting to hug any living, breathing animal who needed her right now and was waiting for her—which would be Kitty. Long gone were the days when Cal acted like he "needed her" in a sexual way, but they had a great marriage nonetheless.

The first thing Jo would do was let Kitty out (again). Although she was housebroken, accidents could happen if Kitty had to wait too long to go out. Jo's mother had repeatedly told her that, as she hated to clean up "accidents," whatever they might consist of.

When Kitty had crapped by the bed, Jo wasn't mad at her, she was furious with Cal. He was the dog person, so he could have prevented the mishap. Jo was going to take care of Kitty like she was a dog person, following the adage, "Learn by Doing." However, she was still against feeding a dog table scraps—for the time being.

Once Kitty was taken care of, Jo wanted to stop by her

mother's and start going through her things. She figured the best approach would be to separate everything between what should be kept, what should be sold, and what should be thrown out. It'd be helpful to have Reg's input, but he'd have to offer it because he detested being told he had to do something, even if it was in the form of a request. As for Cal, he would be happy to help, but he wouldn't dare take any initiative as to what stuff to keep or throw away. Reg had agreed they should sell the house, as he and Jo had both inherited it, and the value of its contents was to be split between them. Jo was proud of their mother for having treated her children equally in her will as obviously Reg and their mother weren't even on speaking terms.

Although Jo's father had made sure his wife was taken care of financially through a generous insurance policy, Jo had no knowledge of an insurance policy of her mother's that named Jo and her brother as beneficiaries. Admittedly she was disappointed, not that Cal and she weren't living comfortably. It was just that in the past couple years, Jo had been daydreaming about Cal and she buying a getaway in Sedona or Flagstaff, so they could escape the tortuous summer heat. She'd wanted to bring up the subject after Brad finally left home, but she hadn't yet gotten around to it. An insurance payout would have provided Jo with an excuse to say something. Cal was always for saving or investing any extra income, including what Jo had been making with her cut-out pictures. Admittedly, however, some of that money had been going toward paying off the mortgage on their house, as there wasn't a penalty if they paid it off early. The insurance money could have gone for a "cabin" up north, they could have paid cash for (provided the insurance payout was in the low to mid six- figures).

Why was she even thinking about this? Jo asked herself. She never was a greedy individual, she just had a certain standard—a lot like her mother. Regarding the latter, she was much lazier, and Constance was relieved her husband had taken care of her financially upon his death, so she would manage to never work a day in her life. That was its own kind of accomplishment.

Frugality wasn't anyone's bag in the Morgan family, although they didn't live beyond their means, either. Reg lived well because he worked hard. Jo sincerely admired him and wished she had more ambition. At least she was "ahead" of her non-ambitious mother. (Jo had no idea why she felt she had to compare herself to her mother, especially considering she was dead.)

Jo considered taking Kitty with her to her mom's house. The biggest issue was whether the dog would fit in her car. Maybe she also needed to consider the possibility she could confuse Kitty by taking her back "home." Truthfully Jo didn't want to go there alone, but it wasn't like she believed in ghosts. Only weirdos believed in the supernatural. Jo prided herself in being as "normal" as anyone could be.

The phone rang. It turned out to be an order for three of her pictures. Just as the woman started describing exactly what she wanted, Jo cut in to say, "I'm sorry, but I can't take any orders right now. I'm on hiatus."

"For how long?" the woman asked.

"I'm not sure," Jo answered. "It's grief-related."

"Oh my. I'm sorry to hear that. Thank you anyway."

Jo thanked the caller in return and couldn't wait to hang up. She'd already had enough of the sympathy that'd been heaped upon her by everyone. As heartened as she was by the overall "goodness of people," she remained skeptical. Maybe the problem was she was looking at herself in the mirror while saying that.

Cal came home from work a few minutes early, only to see Jo's Miata wasn't under the carport. He wasn't worried until going in the kitchen and seeing she hadn't made a single effort to get dinner ready. He'd been hoping she'd begun but needed a couple ingredients and went to the supermarket. One look in her "picture-making room," and it didn't appear she was working on anything. The most puzzling aspect? Kitty was nowhere to be found. The dog's leash was missing, so Jo and Kitty were together, most likely. In all honesty that scenario sounded implausible, but Cal would keep an open mind.

In the meantime, Cal proceeded to kick off his shoes and make himself a drink, compulsively pouring more vodka than he usually did into a tumbler. Not only that he barely diluted it. The day had been so interminable he'd been ready for some alcohol long before quitting time.

After a couple gulps of his drink, Cal felt better—and he had yet to sit down and turn on the television. A couple more swallows and he'd be ready for drink number two, so it was just as well he didn't bother to sit down and relax.

As Cal was mixing drink number two, he felt the alcohol of drink number one continue to flow through him. He again returned to his mother-in-law's death, wondering if his elevated anxiety and stress were because of her. Jo seemed to be handling her mother's death pretty well, considering the fact she was basically OCD-driven. Also, it had to be difficult for her to lose her mother without any warning, so she couldn't at least tell her "good-bye." With her OCD, Jo was undoubtedly dwelling on that issue alone.

Finally Cal sat down and watched the news, second drink in hand. He made a conscious effort to imbibe this one more slowly, not wanting to get soused. Jo detested when he drank too much and honestly preferred he not drink at all. He intended to sit here and wait for Jo (and Kitty) to return home. He couldn't try to call her because she'd left her cell phone on the kitchen counter. That wasn't a cause for concern because she had yet to become obsessed with her phone. Maybe if it was a smartphone the situation would have been different.

Cal had just finished a third drink (weaker than the first two), and his cell phone rang. Fortunately it was on the end table to his right, or he would have had to stand, which might have been impossible to do quickly right at this moment because he was inebriated. He couldn't read the number on the caller I. D., so he went ahead and answered it anyway, only to hear Jo say, "Cal, I'm at Mom's," sounding very weird. Or was he too drunk to hear correctly?

Cal's first question was: "Is Kitty with you?"

"Yes, she is," Jo replied and sounded "more like herself." Then she added, "I came over here to go through some of her things. I even called my brother and he miraculously answered the phone. He said he'd stop by but still had some work to finish. Then he didn't show, so I must have sat in Mom's favorite chair and fell asleep."

Cal hated to be selfish but he was starving, so he remarked, "I wish you would have gotten something ready for dinner before running out the door."

"I'm sorry, Cal," Jo said. "I'd felt a sudden sense of urgency to come over here. It was so bizarre, but like I said, I ended up falling asleep waiting for Reg. Now at least I feel much better. Since Kitty is here with me, I was thinking about spending the night."

"I beg your pardon?"

"I said I was..."

"I heard you just fine, Jo," Cal said, the back of his neck feeling prickly. "I'm frankly astounded you would even verbally entertain the notion of staying at your mother's house for the night when you need to come home and make dinner and...make some pictures."

"I'm officially on hiatus from my creative outlet," Jo proclaimed, back to sounding weird. "I got a call earlier today for a three-picture order, but I turned it down."

"What?"

"I told the woman I was on hiatus and it was grief-related. I felt sorry for her because she sounded like she felt worse than me about my mom's passing. Right now, in fact, I feel great!"

"Are you sure?" Cal asked because the tone of Jo's voice indicated otherwise.

"Yes!" Jo answered. "I'll come home if you want me to, but I'm so comfy here. Maybe I could buy Reg's half of the house, we could sell ours, and we could move here. It's only a few miles, so moving wouldn't be a big deal. And we could finally have a garage!"

Cal honestly could not believe what he just heard. He kept his voice level, telling Jo, "I want you to come home now, Jo. With Kitty. Please."

"All right," she said but didn't sound convinced (or convincing).

"Are you actually on your way right at this moment or are you going to wait on Reg?" Cal asked, not hiding his irritation.

"I'm coming," Jo replied. "I just have to put Kitty in my car. Reg is always waylaid for one reason or another, so he knows I'll understand and do my own thing. I'll call him in the morning and set up a time to meet, hopefully this weekend."

"I can help too, Jo," Cal said. "I know you two need to go through some things together, but I can help with the obvious stuff that's garbage. For now, please just come home!"

Having stated his case, Cal had no expectation of Jo preparing dinner upon her return, given how strange she continued to sound. Fortunately the booze had dulled his appetite, so he was no longer as hungry. He'd wanted to tell Jo he'd order carry-out at an Italian place not far out of her way, and she could pick it up. However, he honestly didn't trust her to make it home if offered a slight detour.

After several agonizing minutes, Jo did indeed return home with Kitty. Both came in the living room wearing shit-eating grins: the latter looked cuter than she already was; the former appeared to have lost her mind (had she?). Luckily Cal had held off making yet another drink, or he might have been too drunk to stand. He was plenty inebriated as it was, and if Jo figured that out, it was possible she would immediately leave again, especially now that she'd decided there was someplace else she'd rather be. Cal actually felt defensive about the fact Jo mentioned wanting to stay at her mother's. Maybe wanting to live there (temporarily) was part of her grieving process. Her talk of wanting to actually move there was just that and nothing more. He'd continue to be as understanding as possible, and hopefully the most intense part of her grieving process would be finished soon.

Reg had wanted to stop by his mother's house when Jo called him to say they should "start going through some things." The problem was he needed more warning (preferably 24 hours). Also, he liked it when she called him in the morning, before he got super busy with the day. However, it was plain she was grief-stricken, so he tried to be as accommodating as possible. Nonetheless, business was business (and he was obsessed with making money), so he put that first. Sure his marriage crumbled because of that mindset, but at least he was rich! He'd make sure to get there over the weekend; Jo knew not to 100% count on an appearance from him on such short notice.

It wasn't as if Reg had a heart of stone; with their mother gone, he had wanted to explain to Jo why he'd estranged himself from her, but his sister didn't feel like listening to him, even alluding to knowing what "it" was. Jo feared hearing something about their mother that painted her in a negative light, but if she too had seen their mother trying to push Dad out of bed one morning when he was having trouble sitting up, Jo's attitude toward their mother would have (hopefully) been quite different.

Reg would continue to wait and be patient for his opportunity to tell Jo why he wouldn't have anything to do with their mother for the decade and a half she was alive after their father's death. At least Jo had Mom's dog to take care of, help her stave off loneliness, as Cal worked forty-plus

141

hours a week—not as much as what Reg put in but worth noting (to Reg). Also, Jo had taken to gluing together some goofy paper cut-out pictures and was actually making some money selling them. Reg had thought Jo was as determined as their mother to never hold a job. Jo was beaten out by Reg's ex-wife, who had no intention of doing anything more than worrying about her well-being, its own full-time (if non-paying) job.

As for Reg and dogs, he had neither the time nor the inclination to care for a furry companion. Lately he seemed to prefer his own company above anything else. He couldn't even get himself to date again. Perhaps dog ownership wasn't too far down the line for him as well.

This weekend Reg planned on making good on his promise to help Jo go through everything in their mother's house. It wasn't like he was blowing Jo off today; he absolutely needed to have more "warning." OCD ran in the family, so his strict adherence to a schedule went without saying. Jo had OCD too, so she was empathetic. Since she was home a lot, having enough outlets for her obsessiveness had to be a challenge, even with her artistic endeavor. If only she knew how much of her brother's ambition was actually OCD-induced, she might not have been as impressed with his accomplishments. As it was their mother never thought much of what Reg had done with his life, career-wise. She didn't even care for his twin sons, Jesse and Taylor. Fortunately they were confident and well-adjusted, so they didn't take it personally. Reg tried not to put "the blame" on his ex-wife, but the fact of the matter was Mother never did approve of his choice of a mate. When Fran started cheating on him, he had to agree.

Reg's kids' names? Those were Fran's idea. Reg had gotten used to them but it had taken years. Just like everything with his ex-wife, she usually got her way, except when he finally wised up and divorced her. (She would have gladly stayed married and continued straying.)

Even divorcing Fran didn't spare Reg from the damage

she'd done. She got the house of his dreams, and it really was. Not only that she got a cash settlement, as there were no child support payments, given the kids' age when the divorce was finalized. The worst part was Jesse and Taylor didn't bother coming home to visit either parent because they were mad at them both. Besides, Fran made no secret of being "done" with them once they left for college, which had to be hurtful.

Someday Reg hoped to clear the air with everyone, attempt to explain his side of each respective "story." He just needed a minute or two of everyone's time. Admittedly he was as stingy as anyone when it came to sparing some time.

Cal could not believe his own wife sometimes, "even after all these years." Although Jo came home from her mother's, almost immediately she went in the backyard (technically a courtyard) with Kitty and sat in one of the patio chairs, staring at the dog. Kitty meandered around, managing to find everything interesting, although watching her couldn't have been that intriguing. What Cal would have given to have had Jo start working on another one of her pictures! He didn't even care if she made dinner by this point. It was dark, yet Jo appeared to be oblivious to that fact. Hopefully by tomorrow she'd realize the importance of her picture-making endeavor: it gave her something constructive to do!

The only "good" part was Jo hadn't appeared to notice how inebriated Cal was. However, he wasn't so out of it he'd forgotten he was hungry earlier in the evening, so he ordered a medium pizza from "Toledo's." Theirs had a very thick crust, three kinds of cheese, and was smothered with tomato sauce. Jo hated it because actually she loved it but knew it was loaded with calories.

Cal ended up whispering the order, as he typically would do because Jo would be in the house. It was like he feared she suddenly had the same hearing as a dog's. He found that so funny he laughed while the woman at the other end of the

143

line was trying to tell him the total. He did manage to hear it, however.

After ending the call, Cal placed his cell phone on the side table and told himself he'd get the money ready for the pizza in a minute. In that time alone he proceeded to fall asleep (or pass out?). When the doorbell rang forty-five minutes after Cal had placed the order, he awoke with a start and was at a loss as to where he was, the time of day, etc. Once he got his bearings (and there was definitely some lag time) he tried to stand but was wobbly because he was drunk.

Meanwhile, here came Jo, Kitty on her heels, both looking like they were answering a fire alarm.

"Who's at the door?" Jo asked, stopping to do so, amazingly enough. Cal told her who it probably was and headed to their bedroom to retrieve his wallet, to which she said, "I'll get the money. My purse is still in the kitchen. How much is it?"

"Twenty-six bucks," Cal replied.

"I'll give the guy thirty-five."

Cal could only nod because he was otherwise speechless. It was amazing Jo would volunteer to pay for anything, let alone include a rather generous tip. Granted, until Jo started creating her pictures, she had no earned income. Nonetheless she was always "thrifty," what he'd loved about her because he was "thrifty," too.

Meanwhile, Kitty sat off to the side, observing the proceedings, looking very much at home, which provided a positive aspect to the evening. In the meantime Cal was still feeling drunk (but famished), and Jo was acting weird.

It was a beautiful Tuesday morning. This was the best time of the year around here, when summer was over but Thanksgiving was still a few weeks away. Cal didn't even need to set the alarm clock to wake up because he was anticipating taking Kitty for a walk before a shower and breakfast (for him). Kitty would just have breakfast. Cal felt like if he didn't hurry up and bond with her, she would become Jo's and only Jo's in no time at all.

Jo was still sleeping, as it was almost an hour earlier than when Cal usually got up. She would be impressed he was taking the initiative to walk her mother's dog. Not only that, he would uphold his promise (to himself) to walk Kitty every morning.

Throwing on a pair of sweatpants and a long-sleeved T-shirt, Cal noticed Jo stirring as if she was about to awaken. Fortunately, she didn't. Otherwise she'd be furious if he awakened her sooner than she was "ready."

Kitty didn't make a single sound on the way out the door, as if she was "in" on Cal's surprise, taking her on a walk so Jo didn't have to bother.

Cal took Kitty for a walk around the block, and the two weren't gone for more than twenty minutes. It was just long enough to be enjoyable but not wear either of them out. As they went back in the house, Cal heard Jo yelling from their bedroom, "Where are you, Cal? Where the hell's Kitty?"

As he was taking off Kitty's leash and petting her, Cal loudly answered, "I'm in the kitchen. I just took Kitty for a walk and now I'm going to feed her."

Not two seconds later (or so it seemed) Jo appeared, barefoot. Something was going on. It was strange enough she swore when asking about Kitty, but the fact she neglected to wear her beloved new slippers? She'd NEVER walk around barefoot in the house.

Glowering at Cal, Jo asked, "Are you basically taking Kitty for yourself? If you are, just say so and quit sneaking around right now!"

"I was just trying to help out," Cal answered. "I'd mistakenly assumed you'd be impressed I'd walked her, so you wouldn't have to feel obligated." It was admittedly very difficult to keep his temper in check, considering he wasn't looking for trouble! Not only that, he truly enjoyed himself walking Kitty and would have had no problem doing so every morning. However, there was indeed a problem, and it concerned Jo. If she hadn't been acting strange already, Cal would have said something was wrong. With her mother having just passed, maybe this was the new normal.

That said, Cal went ahead and fed Kitty, hoping Jo would go back to bed. Maybe if she got another hour of sleep she'd be slightly more reasonable, if temporarily. Maybe their condo wasn't big enough for the three of them (despite the fact it was close to three-thousand square feet). However, Jo's mother's house wasn't more spacious, so they absolutely were not moving there, despite Jo mentioning wanting them to do so.

Jo did not go back to the bedroom and instead continued to stand in the kitchen, arms folded, as she continued to stare at Cal. At this point Cal's head was spinning. Maybe that was better than trying to make sense of it all. Fortunately he was able to leave for work without having an argument with Jo. The two of them hadn't had more than half a dozen major arguments in their 22 years of marriage, but they were admittedly huge (verbal) blow-outs. It was fortuitous they were compatible overall and had the same mindset. Otherwise they most likely would have divorced long ago. Cal liked to think the fact they stayed together, helped give their son stability, as he was evidently a "slow" bloomer. He might never have left home if his parents had split up, especially if he got it in his head his mom needed his company.

It was official (in Cal's head): he would walk Kitty every morning until Jo literally got on her knees and begged him not to do so anymore. (That wasn't an intentional allusion to dogs.) The (potentially) daily outing was far too enjoyable to quit because Jo was worried about Cal "claiming Kitty for himself."

Being the only child of Cal and Jo Greff wasn't exactly easy. Brad had so appreciated how well he'd been provided for, growing up, it was difficult to start college and strike out on his own. Then he started to get a creepy feeling his mother liked having him around, basically doing nothing with himself, not even getting a part-time job. It was nonetheless very alluring to become a bum. Brad's father was the one to thank for getting him off his ass, given how adept the elder Greff was at making incendiary remarks about his son's inertia after graduating from high school.

Out of nowhere Brad pretended to have ambition, which he hoped would generate "real ambition" once he started college in August. He'd chosen a school in Colorado because it was far from home but not too far yet had a much more enjoyable climate. Plus, the scenery was awesome. The fact Barnett Bicycle Institute was in Colorado Springs, on his way to the University of Colorado in Boulder, induced Brad to take a bicycle repair course. He figured with his newfound knowledge he could get a job at a Boulder bike shop. He had to try to support himself, given the fact his parents were paying the first year's tuition and board. He didn't even know what he wanted to major in!

All Brad had been thinking about ever since arriving in Boulder was he never wanted to go home again. The good part was he was able to get a job as a bicycle technician at "Boulder Spokes." The bad part was he soon became a "bicycle bum" and didn't feel like getting out of bed until it was time to go to work—at 4 p.m. He worked five days a week until eight and put in six hours on Saturday. Then on Sundays he'd go out on long rides, sometimes camping and not returning to the dorm until Monday.

In no time at all Brad fell behind in all his classes (he didn't even show up). His whole focus was showing up on time for his job at the bike shop. Any time he wasn't working he was either sleeping or riding his new bicycle, purchased at a huge discount.

After all that, Brad was going home. It was the last place he expected to receive any sympathy, but he wasn't looking for it anyway. What he needed was thirty days to mentally regroup, as outrageous as that sounded. His mom wouldn't mind the layover, but his father would be a different matter. Brad would do what he'd done before: ignore the old man. Ironically his two cousins, Jesse and Taylor, had to deal with hostility from their mother, insofar as not being welcomed back home after leaving for college. Both had graduated a few years ago, as they were older than Brad. However, he was pretty sure neither one had visited their parents more than half a dozen times in a decade. Their situation wasn't helped by the fact their parents had divorced in the meantime.

To say Brad wasn't close to his cousins was an understatement. He received the most information about them from his mother, who got regular updates from her brother Reg, their father. By the time Brad got the news, it was either outdated and/or not even accurate. Brad was well-aware that unless he got on some social media sites, he'd forever be out of the loop with his cousins. Fine with him. He liked technology for the sake of easily getting information, versus using it as a social outlet. Given his age that made zero sense, so there was no place for him in the world. Sometimes he wished he'd been born fifty years earlier than he was. Maybe he wasn't an "old soul," but he was old-fashioned in many ways (unbeknownst to his clueless parents).

On this drive back home, Brad was trusting his aged Honda Civic to get him there. It had gotten him to Boulder, so he'd figured that indicated he would have success. "Higher learning" just wasn't for him. Also, he found that in a new environment he was very anti-social, even worse than he was at home. Working at the bike shop had been his saving grace because he could show up, do his job and keep social interaction to a minimum. The place was so busy he could stay in the back and work on bikes, never having to ring up repair invoices on the register. Although he was aware his anti-social behavior could eventually become problematic, he lived in the here and now. Besides, issue number one was dealing with his dad upon returning home. Dad could "decide" to be cool about Brad's intentions, but he could be an a-hole. The dilemma revolved around the fact his dad was a lazy S.O.B. Brad truthfully detested describing is father as such, accurate though it was. What pissed off Brad the most was the guy acted like he was the CEO of a sophisticated data surveillance company, but he couldn't do anything without specific orders from his supervisor. Although he considered himself a computer whiz, Brad's father didn't know any more about computers than his son. He was basically an ex-hippie who managed not to fry his brain on too many acid trips. That was conjecture, but Brad knew for sure his dad at the very least used to smoke pot because he admitted to as much.

As for Brad, he couldn't stand marijuana. He'd tried it on a couple of occasions, and if what he felt was "the high" pot-heads raved about, he wanted nothing to do with it. All through high school he'd been laughed at for being a teeto-taler and too straight for his own good. He had to hand it to his parents, they were great role models for drug and alcohol abstinence. Overall they weren't bad people, just naive, par-ticularly in regard to their own kid. Even though Brad was "too dumb for college," he was quite perceptive when he would so choose.

Brad hadn't left Boulder until midday, so he was going to get a room for the night and finish the drive in the morning. That way he could return home when his father was at work. His mother would probably be home, but that would be to Brad's benefit. He could talk to her without Dad around, so she would be much more receptive.

Once ensconced in a new-looking but low-budget hotel, Brad determined he should call his mother in the morning before he finished the drive home. Giving her some warning about his imminent arrival would hopefully help bolster her emotional support for him. He certainly wasn't going home to be taken care of financially. If nothing else he could get a job at a bike shop in the Phoenix valley. The last thing Brad wanted to do was disappoint his parents, but maybe there was no avoiding it.

Something brilliant occurred to Brad just as he was about to fall asleep, having spent the evening watching TV: back in Scottsdale he could crash at his grandmother's! His mother had phoned him with the news Grandma Constance had passed away. There was no wake or funeral because she had specified as much. That upset Brad's mother; she felt like Grandma Constance was expressing dislike of her family by not wanting her death "celebrated." Brad thought it was a smart move on his grandma's part, sparing everyone from having to spend money on something she didn't want anyway. Again, he was "too dumb for college," but he liked to think he had some common sense.

Jo was sitting in the courtyard watching Kitty, when her cell phone rang. She didn't usually bring it out here, but obviously it was good she did so. Brad was the caller! He'd never contact her at eleven a.m. unless he had a problem. Sunday evenings around eight had been his preferred time to call her, even if he was on a bicycle trip. The signal was typically iffy, but she was always relieved to hear his voice.

Barely had Jo greeted her son and she was compelled to ask, "Is something wrong?"

"Mom, I'm coming home," Brad replied.

"What?"

"I'm less than an hour away, so don't try to talk me out of it."

Jo couldn't have anyway; she was temporarily speechless. Once she could speak again, she said, "Are you sure you know what you're doing?"

"As far as the decision to quit school? Yes."

"If I may ask, do you have an idea what you're going to do with yourself once you get home?"

"Yes, and I won't be a burden to you and Dad," Brad said. "I know he won't be pleased with how I wasted your money on a semester's worth of classes and a dorm room. I can't guarantee I'll be able to pay you back anytime soon, but I plan on getting a job at a local bike shop. I figure I could crash at Grandma Constance's until you're ready to sell it."

"Are you planning on hiding from your dad for awhile?" Jo wanted to know.

"That wasn't my intention, but now that you mentioned it..."

"He won't be happy to find you're back in town, especially if you can't come up with a good reason why you high-tailed it back home."

"I wanted to at least make it through the semester, but I couldn't stand another day. The whole situation just wasn't for me. I think I could survive college if I could skip the dorm experience. I should have signed up for some classes at ASU and commuted instead."

"You'd wanted to get away from this place in the worst way, Brad! You even said you might not come home again, you liked your new life so much."

"Colorado itself is awesome, Mom. That wasn't the problem. I couldn't tolerate any aspect whatsoever of school. I never mentioned my unhappiness in any phone calls because I didn't want to upset you."

"I'm upset now, how's that?"

Just as Brad started to apologize for as much, the phone line started breaking up, so Jo only heard him say, "I'm losing you, so I'll talk to you when I get home."

Of course Brad might have said good-bye, but it bothered Jo, she didn't actually hear it. Something about the tone of his voice was completely different. It was possible he'd changed in the few months he'd been away, between him attending Barnett Bicycle Institute and then college in Boulder. Or maybe she never knew her own son that well.

"Kitty, let's go inside," Jo said, getting up from the patio chair. She couldn't seem to get her fill of sitting and staring at Kitty, a favorite "activity" of her mother's.

Amy Kristoff

Soon Brad would be "home from college" but nothing like Jo had previously imagined. She'd honestly thought he'd "stay away" until he had a four-year degree. His father would not be pleased. Beyond that Jo had no idea how Cal might "react," so maybe it was good if Brad temporarily lived in his grandmother's house. However, Jo would be sure to tell Reg his nephew was staying there, in case he stopped by on a whim to go through some of Mom's things.

The most important part was to warn Reg to not let Cal know Brad was living there. As far as Cal, Jo would deal with him in due time. Cal was easygoing, but lately he'd been referring to Brad as "the kid," which indicated no optimism whatsoever for their son and his future. At the same time, the last thing Cal would expect was to have his son abruptly quit school.

"Is it time for your lunch?" Jo asked Kitty while the former was looking in the kitchen cabinets, deciding what she needed before going to the supermarket. Meanwhile, Kitty sat on her haunches, patiently waiting for her food. "Your food is in the walk-in pantry behind us, so I'll get it in just a second." Typically Jo didn't write a grocery list, but lately she couldn't seem to remember anything, other than some items specifically for Brad: a box of macaroni and cheese as well as a head of iceberg lettuce to make a salad drenched with vinegar and oil dressing and covered with croutons. At least her son was easy to please. Maybe she'd whip up a meal for him before his dad came home from work. It might even be kind of exciting having her son "hiding out," temporarily. He had a house key, so if he came home before she returned from the store, he could let himself in. She'd leave a note on the kitchen counter, telling him where she went and that Kitty was present. In all the confusion, she hadn't told him about taking over the care of Grandma Constance's dog.

Meanwhile, Kitty continued to sit on her haunches, patiently waiting for lunch. Finally Jo completed opening and closing about every kitchen cabinet, expending nervous ener-

152

gy more than accomplishing anything. "I'll get your lunch right now, Kitty," Jo told the dog. Then she paused, realizing she really was talking to a dog! It didn't bother her per se, but what creeped her out was the inescapable feeling she was becoming her mother—literally. This was far more invasive than yet another daughter "becoming just like her mother." It almost felt physical.

With Kitty fed (she ate in about three seconds), Jo grabbed a pen and paper and scribbled down some items for her grocery list. Then she wrote a note to Brad. Only when she'd completed both did she realize she hadn't washed her hands after touching Kitty's bowl. She started howling with laughter upon being aware of as much. Either she really was becoming her mother or she lost her mind. Neither one bothered her; in fact, she felt like celebrating. Maybe she was sick and tired of who she was before. To think, she came to that realization thanks to a dog!

Cal was glad to be home, he thought as he pulled into the driveway, although Jo's Miata was missing. Where the hell was she off to now? He'd much rather have to tear her away from her picture-making than conjecture about her whereabouts. He was willing to bet she never made another picture, as it appeared her interest in the activity had ended with the death of her mother.

Then Cal went inside and upon reaching the kitchen he saw a note with Jo's handwriting on the kitchen counter: "Brad: I ran to the store to pick up some things. Wait here and I'll whip something up before you go to Grandma Constance's. Love, Mom. P.S. Kitty's here, so give her a pat and let her out in back if you want—just make sure the gate's shut!"

Looking around for Kitty, Cal hoped she was with Jo after all because she wasn't here and the gate was wide open. He was going to plant his butt in his favorite chair and get drunk. Doing so made time pass more quickly. As for Brad,

Cal was really going to let him have it for quitting school.

Reg had a few extra minutes this evening to go through some of Mom's things, so he went to her house, not even telling Jo he would be doing so. She was annoying, how she wanted to know when he'd be there, as if she was afraid to be alone. She always was different, something Reg hesitated to admit.

As soon as Reg unlocked the front door of Mom's house, he swore his mother asked, "Reg, is that you?" Afterward she emitted a cackle-laugh that made every hair on his body stand on end. Immediately he shut the door and locked it with the key, a nearly-impossible feat because his hands were shaking so much. He'd call Jo in the morning and tell her she could have the house and its entire contents. She never thought things were "even" between them, anyway.

"We did it, Kitty," Jo said. "All I had to do was hide my car in the garage and scaredy-cat Reg ran away. Two down, one to go. And Cal has a key, so I won't have to leave the door unlocked like I did for Brad."

Amy has written several novels and short story collections, including *Retribution and Other Twisted Tales* in 2016 and *Dogs and Their Twisted Tales* in 2017. She resides on a horse farm in Indiana. AmyKristoff.com.